HOUSE OF THE DEAD

MURDER FORCE BOOK 4

ADAM J. WRIGHT

Copyright © 2022 by Adam J. Wright

All rights reserved.

No part of this book may be reproduced in any form or by any electronic or mechanical means, including information storage and retrieval systems, without written permission from the author, except for the use of brief quotations in a book review.

The locations in this book are real. Some details may have been changed for story purposes.

For my father, Kenneth Wright.

THE MURDER FORCE SERIES

THE MURDER FORCE SERIES

EYES OF THE WICKED

SILENCE OF THE BONES

REMAINS OF THE NIGHT

HOUSE OF THE DEAD

ECHO OF THE PAST

THE WIDOW MAKER

OTHER BOOKS BY ADAM J. WRIGHT

Psychological Thrillers:

DARK PEAK (DCI Battle)

THE RED RIBBON GIRLS (DI Summers)

Urban Fantasy:

THE HARBINGER PI SERIES

LOST SOUL

BURIED MEMORY

DARK MAGIC

DEAD GROUND

SHADOW LAND

MIDNIGHT BLOOD

TWILIGHT HEART

FAERIE STORM

NIGHT HUNT

GRAVE NIGHT

FINAL MAGIC

CHAPTER
ONE

The flash drive arrived in a nondescript, brown padded envelope. The name and address were printed on the front in black capital letters.

Superintendent Gallow
  Murder Force
  York

There was just enough information for the package to be delivered to the old school building that now served as the Murder Force headquarters.

There was no return address.

The desk sergeant on duty the day the package arrived—DS Freeman—eyed the envelope suspiciously and rang up to the third floor, where Gallow's office was situated. The superintendent was not in the building at the moment, however, and the desk sergeant knew this.

"Flowers," a voice on the other end of the line said when Freeman's call was answered.

"Matt, it's Carl on the front desk. I've got a package here for the super."

"He's not in today. Just send it up to his office with the rest of the post."

"I could do that, yeah, but it's a bit funny, this one. No return address and barely anything written on the front.

"Got your spidey sense tingling, has it?" Matt Flowers asked.

"You could say that, yeah. Do you think someone should have a look at it?"

Flowers didn't say anything for a moment, then asked, "Are you really that worried about it, Carl?"

Freeman looked at the envelope in front of him. He couldn't put his finger on it, but something about it felt…off.

"I'd like a second opinion. I wouldn't feel right letting it through."

"All right, I'll be down in a minute." Flowers hung up.

Two minutes later, he was pushing through the door into reception. He shot Freeman a quick smile. "Right, what have we got?"

Freeman placed the brown envelope on the desk between them.

Flowers frowned at it. "Looks innocent enough.

Not much of an address on the front." He turned it over. "Nothing at all on the back."

Squeezing the envelope gingerly, he said, "Something small inside. Hand me that letter opener."

"Are you sure?" Carl said. "Making a safety assessment is one thing, but we shouldn't open the superintendent's mail. Perhaps we should give him a ring. See if he's expecting anything."

"He's golfing in Scotland at the moment. Do *you* want to interrupt his game?"

"Well, no, I suppose not."

"And we can't just take it up to his office. There could be anything in it."

"Like what? It's too small to be a bomb."

"Like a listening device. We discuss high-profile cases up there. What if a reporter sent it to get a scoop on the latest cases? Or find out personal info on our people?"

"I hadn't thought of that." He handed Flowers the letter opener.

"But what if it's something the super is expecting? He'll be fuming if he finds out you opened it."

"Let me deal with that." Flowers slid the letter opener's blade into the envelope and cut a small opening at one end. He held the envelope up and looked inside before sliding the contents into his hand.

A small, black, plastic flash drive sat in his palm.

"Is that all?" Freeman asked. "No letter or anything?"

Flowers checked the envelope. "Nothing. I'm

taking this upstairs. Good job, Carl." He took the flash drive and the envelope to the door.

"Thanks." Freeman wasn't sure why he was being thanked, but he accepted it gracefully.

Flowers used his access card to re-enter the main part of the building and disappeared up the stairs.

———

Matt took the flash drive to the IT department. He walked past the technicians at their desks and went straight to Chris Toombs' office.

Toombs was leaning back in his chair, staring at a screen in front of him when Matt walked in. "Hey," he said. "It's Matt, right? How can I help you?"

"This just arrived in the mail." Matt held out the flash drive. "I think someone should have a look at it."

"No problem. We'll open it on the Brick."

"The Brick?"

"It's a computer that isn't connected to any of our networks. It isn't connected to anything at all. Totally isolated. So, if there's a virus on this thing, we won't catch it."

He led Matt out of the office and into another room, which seemed to be a storeroom for printer paper and stationery, except for the fact that a small table sat against one wall and a laptop sat on the table.

The laptop had a black plastic cover on its lid and someone—probably Toombs himself—had painted the word *BRICK* on it in white paint.

The technician opened the laptop and booted it up. He took the flash drive from Matt and inserted it into the machine.

"There's just a single text file," he said. "Weird."

"What does it say?"

Toombs clicked the file. It opened and Matt leaned in closer to get a better look. There was nothing but a string of numbers and letters.

"It's a website address," Toombs said. "Probably a link, but we can't click on it because we're on the Brick." He grabbed a sticky note and a pen from one of the shelves and copied the string of characters and numerals.

He closed the file and removed the flash drive from the Brick. He gave the drive back to Matt. "We won't need this anymore. There's a laptop in my office that's connected to the Net via a dongle and isn't connected to our network. We can visit this website safely on that."

"A computer for every occasion," Matt said as they went back to Toombs' office.

"Can't be too careful nowadays," the technician said. "Who was this drive addressed to?"

"Gallow."

"So, it might be nothing more sinister than his holiday snaps?"

"It's possible."

"If he spent his summer at a nudist colony, we'll never be able to unsee this."

Flowers laughed. "I don't think it's anything like that."

When they got to Toombs' office, the technician removed a laptop from his desk drawer and turned it on. He sat in his chair and invited Matt to pull up one of the spares that were arranged around a small meeting table by the wall.

Matt sat in a chair and wheeled himself over to Toombs' desk.

"Okay, here we go." Toombs stuck the note to the top of the screen and opened an Internet browser. He typed in the long string of numbers and letters.

When he hit the *Enter* key, the screen went black for a second, and then words began to appear one by one, in a red font that dripped animated blood.

Will the police save them?

Matt frowned at the words. "Save who?"

A white square appeared on the screen, with more words—also in white—underneath it.

Family Get Together

"What's that supposed to mean?" Matt said.

"It's a clickable link." Toombs clicked the square and it expanded to fill the screen.

They were now looking at a black and white video that showed four people sitting at a dining table in a house. The words *Live Feed* glowed in the top right of the screen.

The feed itself—if that's what it was and not a

recording—was being filmed from the corner of the family's dining room.

The father sat at the head of the table. He was facing away from the camera and had dark hair. The mother was blonde and sat at the opposite end of the table. Her face was a mask of terror.

The children seated at the table looked to be a blonde-haired girl aged around eight and a dark-haired boy who was facing away from the camera. The girl's eyes were wide and she looked terror-stricken, like her mother.

Matt wasn't sure why until he looked closer. Wires trailed across the floor beneath the family, snaking up to the underside of the table, where some kind of device seemed to have been fixed.

"That looks like a bomb," Toombs said.

Matt gritted his teeth and checked the room for some clue—anything—that would tell him where this was taking place. His eyes followed the dark tangle of wires and he realized they were attached to the house's front door, which was visible from the dining room through an archway.

"Is this actually live?" he asked Toombs. "Can you tell?"

The technician raised his shoulders and hands in a helpless gesture. "I don't know."

Matt pulled his phone from his pocket and rang DI Summers. "We have a problem," he said as soon as she picked up. "I'm in the IT office and I'm watching a family about to get blown up."

Dani simply said, "On my way," and hung up.

"There are other people watching this," Toombs said, pointing at a view counter that had appeared at the bottom right of the screen. As Matt watched, the counter moved from *1,341* to *1,457*.

"We need to know where this is coming from," Matt said.

"Already on it." Toombs was on his desktop computer, typing numbers and code into it.

A smaller inset window appeared over the video feed. This window showed a street and appeared to be shot from a front door. The words *Live Feed* showed in the top right of this window as well.

As Matt watched, police cars pulled up outside the house. Uniformed officers got out and ran up the path to the door, their faces almost looking into the lens as they knocked.

"Must be a doorbell camera," Toombs said.

On the main feed, the family at the table looked towards the door. There was no sound, but it was obvious they could hear the police outside.

In the small window, an officer was taking the big red key—the metal ram the police used to batter down doors—from the boot of his car.

"No!" Matt shouted helplessly at the screen. Somewhere, the police were about to make entry into a house and trigger a bomb and there was nothing he could do to stop it.

The big red key was brought to the door and the officer holding it brought it back before swinging it forwards.

The feed that showed the family went suddenly

white and then showed only static. The image from the doorbell camera shook and showed the officers being blown backwards towards the road before it, too, broadcast nothing more than static.

The door opened and DI Summers entered, her face concerned. "Matt, what's happening?"

"It's too late," Matt said grimly. "They're all dead."

CHAPTER TWO

"Tell me again about the flash drive and how it got here," Dani said to Matt. They were sitting in one of the meeting rooms, beneath a fluorescent ceiling light that Dani found too bright.

The envelope and the flash drive had been sent to the lab for testing.

"There's nothing much to tell, Guv," Matt said. "DS Freeman received the package at the front desk and was suspicious of it, so I opened it and took the drive to Toombs. That's how we found the website and the feed. If that's what it was."

"We're checking," she said. The question that kept running through her mind was why. Why would someone send them the video?"

Her phone buzzed on the table. She picked it up. "Summers."

"Hi, this is Cathy from the admin team. I've been looking into the request you put in earlier regarding searching for reports of an explosion today."

"Yes," Dani said. She wanted the girl to get to the point.

"There was an explosion earlier today at a house in York. It's all over the news. They're sifting through the rubble now."

"How many people were hurt?" Dani gripped the phone tightly. She already knew she wasn't going to like the answer.

"Early reports indicate four people inside the house and three police officers were found dead at the scene. Two officers were rushed to hospital and another three suffered minor injuries."

Seven people dead. "Is there anything else? Has anyone claimed responsibility? Is it a terrorist attack?"

"That's all we know at the moment, I'm afraid. It's still early days. It's only just happened."

She wanted to shout, *Yes, I know it just happened. Two people in my team had to* watch *it happen*, but instead, she said, "Right. Thank you, Cathy," and hung up.

"Everything all right, Guv?" Matt asked, detecting the frustration in her voice. They'd worked together for a long time and could read each other easily.

"Seven people dead at the scene, Matt, and two more taken to hospital."

"Jesus."

"I don't understand the live feed. Why send it to us?"

"Well, technically, it was sent to Superintendent Gallow."

"But he *is* us. He's the face of Murder Force that everyone sees on TV."

"Maybe the Doc can figure out why someone sent it to us."

"Tony's still on leave." The forensic psychologist had taken a couple of days off because his girlfriend was visiting him from an archaeological dig in Sussex.

Dani's phone buzzed again. The screen said, *Battle*.

"Sir," she said as she answered.

"Have you heard what's happened?"

She could hear traffic in the background. It sounded like the DCI was driving.

"If you mean the explosion—"

"Of course I mean the explosion. It's all over the bloody news. I'm on my way there now. I want you to get over here as well. 34 Winsall Road. The media are crawling all over this. That makes it a high-profile case, so now it's been dropped into our laps. I don't think Counter-Terrorism is too happy about that, but it is what it is."

"There's more to it as well," she said. "The explosion was broadcast live on the Net. Someone sent us a link."

"What? Right, tell me the details when you get here." He ended the call.

"I'm going down there," Dani told Matt. "Battle is already on his way. Check in with Toombs. See if he's worked out where that site is being broadcast from."

He nodded. "All right, guv."

She left the meeting room and collected her coat and bag before going downstairs. She approached Carl Freeman on the front desk. "I'm going to need a full report about that package that arrived earlier," she told him.

Freeman—who obviously didn't know what had been on the flash drive—nodded and said, "Yes, ma'am."

Dani went outside, crossed the car park to her Land Rover and got in behind the wheel. The weight of frustration sat on her shoulders, and it wasn't only because her team had been targeted by whatever sicko had carried out this crime.

She knew that this was just the beginning. Setting up a website, posting a flash drive, and broadcasting the crime over the Net didn't feel like a one-time thing. Whoever was behind this had planned it out meticulously and got the result they wanted. There was no doubt in her mind that they would do it again, and more lives would be lost.

She tried to put that out of her mind as she drove out of the car park and through the industrial estate on the road that led to town. She could only focus on what was in front of her, not on what was going to happen in an unknown future.

That thought didn't make her feel any better.

They would be scrambling in the dark trying to solve this while the killer would know exactly what was going to happen next, where he would strike from the darkness.

She used the hands-free to call Matt. Maybe he had some good news. Toombs was an expert in all things digital, so perhaps he'd uncovered something.

"Guv," the DS said when he answered, his voice coming from the Land Rover's speakers.

"Tell me you've got something, Matt."

"Nothing so far, guv. It's all foreign proxy servers and rerouted IP addresses. It doesn't mean much to me, but Chris says our man has basically erased his digital footprints."

Dani gritted her teeth in frustration. They were dealing with a computer pro. This case had just become much more difficult.

"All right," she said. "Let me know if anything turns up."

"Will do, guv."

She arrived at Winsall Road to find the entire area cordoned off. Beyond the police tape, firemen were spraying water over the charred remains of what had once been a family home.

She made her way through the throng of reporters and television cameras and showed her ID to the uniform standing guard at the tape. He waved her through.

The residents of Winsall Road had been evacuated. The only people on the street were the firefighters, several uniformed police officers, and Battle.

"Summers," he said. "You'd better tell me about this link we were sent. I've got Counter-Terrorism breathing down my neck, telling me this case should be theirs. What's our connection to it?"

"A flash drive arrived at HQ with a link to a website that showed a live feed from inside the house. Matt Flowers and Chris Toombs saw the whole thing."

"Bloody hell. What kind of sick-minded individual does that? It's bad enough that they killed a family of innocent people—and three of ours—without filming it as well."

"I don't know, guv."

"I assume this flash drive is being analysed by the lab."

Dani nodded. "And the envelope it came in."

"And that's all we've got as far as leads go?"

"That's all so far. Anything this end?" She gestured to the remains of number 34.

"Not yet. They've only just put the fire out. Someone will have a look at the bomb and try to work out how it was made, but there isn't much else to go on. The uniforms are taking statements from the neighbours in the hopes someone saw something suspicious. I'm not holding out much hope. If he's clever enough to do this, he won't have been blundering down the street in plain sight of the curtain twitchers."

"Toombs is looking for a digital footprint

regarding the website, but he hasn't found anything so far."

"So, we're dealing with someone who's a wizard at computers and also knows how to build bombs," Battle mused. "This isn't going to be easy."

"Inspector Battle?" said a male voice behind them.

They both turned to see a tall dark-haired man dressed in black trousers and a dark blue jumper approaching from the direction of the tape.

"Who's asking?" Battle said.

"Ian Radcliffe. Counter-Terrorism." The man held out his hand and Battle shook it reluctantly.

"This is our case, Radcliffe," the DCI said. "The perpetrator has made contact with my team."

Radcliffe looked surprised. "Really? How has he done that?"

"He sent us a flash drive with a link to his website."

"Wow, okay. Look, I'm not here to take the case off you. I've had a word with my superior and we've agreed that I should offer my services to you. Work alongside your people. If it turns out that this is a terrorist attack, then I have expertise that could be useful."

"You want to become part of my team, do you?" Battle said suspiciously.

"Temporarily, yes."

"And you say your superior agreed to this?"

"Yes."

"I *will* check, you know."

Radcliffe grinned. "I have no doubt you will. Inspector."

Battle looked the man up and down and then nodded slowly. "All right. But until I've checked with your boss and made sure this is all above board, I want you back behind that tape."

"Understood," Radcliffe said. He turned and went back to the cordon.

Dani's phone buzzed. She took it out of her pocket and said to Battle, "It's Matt."

"Put him on speaker."

She answered the call. "Matt, you're on speaker. I'm here with the DCI."

"There's been a development," Matt said. He sounded worried.

"Out with it, man," Battle said.

"Another feed has appeared on the website. It isn't clickable yet, and it doesn't show anything, but there's a timer above it. It started counting down at five hours. Now, it's at four hours and fifty-seven minutes."

"He's not giving us time to solve this crime before he commits the next," Dani said.

"Right, I want everyone at headquarters in the next half hour," Battle said. "Where's Sheridan?"

"He's on holiday, guv," Dani said.

"Not anymore, he's not."

CHAPTER
THREE

Tony Sheridan sat by the window of *Sam's Café* in the Bootham district of York and finished his tea. Earlier, he'd heard the wail of sirens in the distance, but they were quiet now. He put the empty mug on the table next to the plate that his all-day breakfast had been on ten minutes ago, before he'd wolfed it down in record time.

"You made short work of that," Alina said. She'd opted for a cheese baguette and still had some of it left on her plate. Tony eyed it for a moment, wondering if she was going to finish it and if he still had room for it, if she wasn't.

Deciding that he did indeed have room for the remains of the baguette, he shifted his eyes up to meet hers.

"Were you looking at my food?" she asked suspiciously.

"No, not really."

She narrowed her dark eyes at him.

"I was just wondering if you were going to finish it," he admitted.

She pushed the plate across the table towards him. "You can have it."

"You sure?"

She nodded. "I'm full, anyway. Breakfast was more than enough for me."

He'd made a huge stack of blueberry pancakes this morning and they'd sat at his kitchen table—he in his pyjama bottoms, she in one of his old shirts, which he thought looked incredibly sexy on her—and eaten the lot smothered with maple syrup and butter.

They had plans to visit the *Jorvik Viking Centre* later. Tony was already wondering—even as he popped the remains of Alina's baguette into his mouth—if there might be a restaurant or café there.

His phone rang in his pocket. He fished it out and checked the screen

Dani.

"It's work," he told Alina. "Not sure why they're ringing me." He wasn't due back until the day after tomorrow, when Alina went back to Sussex.

"You should answer it and find out," she said.

He supposed she was right, although he didn't want to be dragged into work while Alina was here had a sneaking suspicion—mainly because of the sirens he'd heard wailing from somewhere in the city—that Dani was calling for more than a friendly chat.

However, he couldn't ignore the call, even if he

was on holiday. With a sigh of resignation, he put the phone to his ear and said, "Hi, Dani."

"Tony, something's come up. Battle wants you at HQ in half an hour."

"Oh." His suspicions had been confirmed. He and Alina wouldn't be looking at Vikings this afternoon.

"I know Alina's visiting," Dani said, "and I'm sorry. But this really is important."

Tony sighed again. "All right, I'll be there." He ended the call.

"You have to go in to work," Alina guessed.

He nodded and reached across the table to take her hand. "I'm sorry. Look, it might not take long, whatever it is."

"If it's anything to do with those sirens we heard, it is not a minor matter, Tony. They wouldn't bring you in from your holiday if it was nothing."

"I know. But we had plans."

"We can go to the Viking Centre another time. I'll take the opportunity to go shopping. You hate waiting around for me in shops, and I need some new boots. The Sussex mud has ruined my old ones."

He handed her his keyring. "Here's the key to the flat. In case I'm not back until later."

She took it and nodded. "I'll get us something for dinner. Let me know when you're coming home, and I'll have it ready."

"Do you want me to drop you in town?" he asked, getting up from the table.

"I'll get a taxi. You should go; they'll be waiting."

Wondering how he could be so lucky to have such an understanding girlfriend, he leaned over to kiss her and left the café. His Mini was parked across the street.

He climbed in and was about to switch the radio to a local station to see what was going on, when he discovered there was no need; the event had made the national news.

"...An explosion in York that has killed seven people. Police haven't released the victims' names, and have not confirmed if the explosion is a terrorist attack, although reports are coming in that an explosive device has been removed from the scene. A press conference will be held later today."

Tony hoped to hear more details as he drove across the city, but the radio station didn't divulge any. By the time he arrived at headquarters, Tony was none the wiser regarding the cause of the explosion or who the victims were.

"Hello, Carl," he said to the desk sergeant as he entered the building. "I haven't got my card on me. Can you buzz me in?"

"Of course, Dr Sheridan." DS Freeman pressed a button under the desk and Tony was allowed into the inner part of the building.

He went up the stairs to the second floor, where Battle and the others would be waiting. He hadn't made it in the thirty minutes Dani had specified, but he was no more than five minutes late.

Still, that didn't deter Battle from saying, "Dr Sheridan, so good of you to join us," when Tony entered the meeting room.

The room was full of detectives and uniformed officers sitting on plastic chairs, facing front. The DCI stood before them, next to a whiteboard. Tony scanned the information on the board—which Battle had written in blue marker—to bring himself up to speed.

34 Winsall Road
Thompson family
Father - Luke
Mother - Wendy
Children - Laura (8), Dylan (10)
Device beneath dining table
Trigger on front door
Three officers killed when attempting to make entry
Broadcast on Internet
Link sent to Supt Gallow
Next crime 1600 hours

"As I was saying," the DCI said, addressing the room, "we don't know why he's doing this, or why he sent that flash drive to this building. Is he showing off? Gloating? Dr Sheridan, I assume you've been told the details of the case. Can you shed any light on why someone would do this?"

All eyes in the room turned to look at Tony expectantly.

"Actually, I only know what's written on that board," Tony admitted. "What's this about it being broadcast on the Internet?"

CHAPTER THREE 23

"A live feed of the entire thing was posted online," Chris Toombs said from a seat near the front.

"So, he obviously wants an audience," Tony said. "He could be showing off, or there could be more to it. He might have a message that he wants to get out there. Is this terrorist related?"

"Not as far as we know," Battle said.

"He hasn't sent any demands? Posted any messages with some sort of agenda?"

"Only the videos," Toombs said.

"He hasn't said he'll strike again at four o' clock? The board says the next crime will be at 1600 hours."

The IT computer looked grim. "He hasn't said so in so many words. Another video is due to appear then. There's a timer on the website." He held up his phone. Tony could see white digits counting down.

4:18.21

As he watched the 21 seconds counted down to 14 seconds.

"May I?" he asked Toombs, going to the front of the room. Toombs gave him the phone. Tony saw the caption *Will the police save them?* at the top of the webpage.

"Probably someone with a grudge against the police," he said. "Trying to show the audience that the police couldn't do anything to save the Thompson family."

"Of course they couldn't," Battle said, "he'd

rigged the explosives to the front door. As soon as the officers opened it, the house went up."

"So, his message is that the police couldn't save this family, and he made sure that was the case by ensuring the Thompsons were killed."

"We never said we could save everyone," the DCI said. "What's his problem?"

"I don't know," Tony said, handing the phone back to Toombs.

"And what's he going to do at four o' clock?"

"Probably more of the same. He's made his point. Now, he'll want to reinforce it."

"Bloody hell," Battle said frustratedly. "I want everyone ready to move. He got the police over to Winsall Road by leaving an anonymous tip that a family was in danger inside. If a similar tip comes in around four o' clock, I'll be informed. Until then, I want you all to be vigilant. Those of you on patrol this afternoon, look for anything suspicious, especially in residential areas. If you think something looks wrong, or someone expresses concern about a neighbour they've not seen all day, get on it. Check it out."

He turned to the IT technician. "Toombs, I want you and Dr Sheridan to watch the feed again. Let us know what's going on inside the house."

"No problem," Toombs said. "I'll record it as well, in case we need to review the footage later. Could be some clues on there."

"Good idea. Everyone else, be ready to get over to the scene. We're not going to make entry until we know it's safe for our officers and the family inside. The bomb squad is on alert. We'll have to wait for them to defuse any devices before we enter the house. Is everyone clear on what they're doing?"

Everyone in the room nodded their understanding and some murmured in the affirmative.

Tony understood his role but felt a tight ball of anxiety rise from his stomach up to his throat. If this all went wrong, he would witness a family die in real time. That was something he knew he'd never be able to scrub from his mind.

The room emptied slowly, the officers talking among themselves as they went back to their desks and patrol duties.

Battle came over and said to Toombs, "What's the chance of you cracking where that website came from and finding this bastard's address before four o' clock?"

"Zero," the technician said bluntly. "He's hidden his tracks too well."

Battle's face was grim. "Right. We'll just have to hope we can save the next family, then." He left the room.

"He wasn't too happy about that," Toombs said to Tony.

"He understands you can't perform miracles. He just wants to catch this guy before anyone else gets hurt."

"Don't we all." He checked the timer on his phone. "I suppose I should keep trying, even though it won't do any good. At least it'll keep me busy and not worrying about what's going to happen in a few hours. You're welcome to join."

"I'll be there in a bit," Tony said. He needed to ring Alina and let her know he was going to be home late.

He left the meeting room and leaned against the window at the end of the hallway, looking out at the industrial estate while he called her.

"Tony," she said. "I heard about it on the news. How terrible."

"Yeah, it's a bad one. I'm going to be late tonight. This thing is still ongoing. Don't wait for me before you eat, or anything."

"Of course I will wait. You just get home when you can. And safely, please."

He smiled. He wasn't used to having someone care about him. "I'll be fine. See you later."

"All right. See you."

He hung up and went in search of coffee. He had a jar of instant in the cupboard in the staff kitchen, but he needed something stronger. In the canteen downstairs, they had a proper machine, and the coffee was tasty and strong.

He went down and bought two Americano coffees to take away. One for himself and one for Toombs. He didn't even know if the technician liked coffee but assumed he would. Toombs seemed rather Americanised in his ways, and that probably included drinking coffee over tea.

He went up to IT and found the technician tapping away on his keyboard in his office.

"Brought you a coffee," Tony said, holding up the cardboard cup.

"Thanks, man." Toombs took the cup and placed it on the desk next to him.

The screen in front of him was filled with computer code. Tony didn't understand any of it.

A laptop sat next to the desktop computer with the *Will the police save them?* website showing on its screen. The timer said, *3:47.04*.

Tony left the office and went upstairs to get a notebook and pen from his desk drawer.

He found Dani poring over a list of names and mugshots on her computer.

"Hey, Tony," she said as he opened his desk drawer and began rifling through it. "Sorry you had to cut your holiday short."

"It's fine. I wouldn't want to be left out on this one. He's targeting our own people, and I take that personally."

He found an A4 notebook and tossed it on the desk before resuming his search of the drawer, this time for a pen.

"What are you doing?" he asked, Dani, nodding at the row of mugshots on her screen.

"Looking for criminals with a hatred of the police and a high degree of skill with computers and explosives."

"I imagine that list is quite long." He found a black biro and held it up triumphantly.

"What are you up to?" Dani joked. "Writing your memoirs?"

"Finding out what makes this guy tick."

"There's not a lot to go on."

"There's enough to make a start. It's all in the details. *He* is in the details."

"Like the devil."

"Precisely." He slid into his chair and opened the notebook. At the top of the page, in capital letters, he wrote, *WHO IS HE?*

Below that, he wrote the word *FACTS* and listed what was known for a fact regarding the unknown subject of their investigation.

Family annihilator

Police killer

Computer skills

Explosive skills

Male

These were cold, hard facts about the person they were looking for, and could all be gleaned from the videos, the website, and the phone call to the police.

Tony then made a second list further down the page. These were questions that couldn't be answered with any certainty yet.

Why broadcast the crimes?

What message is he trying to convey?

Why the Thompson family in particular?

How did he choose the family?

"Is someone looking into the Thompson family?" he asked Dani.

"Yeah, Matt and Lorna are on it. Why? Have you got something?"

"I was just wondering how he found them."

"If there was any contact between him and the family recently, Matt and Lorna will find it."

"Yeah." He looked back down at his list and wondered if the Thompson family fit this man's message in a specific way, or if any family would suit his purposes.

He supposed, grimly, that he'd know more about that when the second family was revealed. He looked up at the clock on the wall. Unless one of the patrols had a lucky break soon, another family would die soon.

A dark-haired man Tony didn't recognise sat down at the desk opposite. He saw Tony looking at him and smiled. "Hi, I'm Ian Radcliffe. Counter Terrorism." He stood up and held his hand out over the low partition that separated their desks.

Tony shook it. Radcliffe had a strong grip. "Tony Sheridan. You're barking up the wrong tree."

Radcliffe raised an eyebrow. "Excuse me?"

"This isn't an act of terrorism," Tony said. "There are no demands, no group taking responsibility. This isn't a large-scale event that takes place on the streets. It's contained. Targeted. Too specific to be a terrorist attack."

"Well, we can't be certain of anything yet."

Tony went back to his lists and added the word, *Terrorism?*. "Was the Thompson family politically active in some way?" he asked Radcliffe. "Could blowing up their house be considered a political statement?"

Radcliffe shook his head. "They didn't have any strong political ties or views," he admitted.

Tony crossed the word *Terrorism?* out.

Radcliffe sat down and opened a laptop. He started working on it.

Tony examined the notebook page. He couldn't put a profile together from the scant lists of facts and questions, and it was too early to start making suppositions.

After half an hour of staring at the paper and coming up with nothing, he sat back in his chair and admitted defeat. He wasn't going to crack the case with the information he had in front of him.

He got up and went to the window, looking out over the industrial estate and, beyond that, the city of York. The man they were after was out there somewhere, putting together the four o' clock broadcast. Who the hell was he and what did he want?

He pulled his phone out of his pocket and rang Matt Flowers.

"Hello, Doc," Flowers said when he answered. "What can I do for you?"

"Tell me about the Thompson family."

"Not a lot to tell, really. Luke Thompson was a chartered accountant. Wendy was a manager at a local supermarket. The kids were doing all right at school. Just a regular family."

"No skeletons in any closets?"

"Not as far as we can see. Neighbours and work

colleagues all say the same thing: the Thompsons were a normal, likeable family."

Tony sighed. This wasn't going to be easy. "Thanks, Matt."

"No problem, Doc."

Tony ended the call and went back to his desk. He added the words, *Normal family* to his list and wondered how they'd come into contact with the man who would broadcast their deaths on the Internet.

Perhaps he'd been a disgruntled customer at the supermarket where Wendy worked, or maybe he was a client of Luke's and was unhappy with his tax return.

There were too many possibilities. Once he knew who the next target was, connections could be made, but until then—as much as he hated to admit it—he was in the dark.

He went back down to Toombs' office and discovered that the coffee he'd left there was, not unsurprisingly, cold.

Toombs was still typing code into his computer. As Tony moved the cup of cold coffee aside, the technician looked over at the laptop and said, "Whoa, that's new."

Tony squinted at the laptop. Above the second square, beneath the timer—which now read, *1:58.12* —were the three words in a stark, white font.

Family Tea Party.

CHAPTER
FOUR

"Any more developments?" Battle stuck his head into Toombs' office. Tony knew the DCI was hoping for any kind of break or clue and he felt frustrated that he had no new information to give the man.

Since the appearance of the title over the second square, the website hadn't changed, other than the timer, which now said, *0:22.10*

Twenty-two minutes left.

Toombs had been typing away like a man possessed, and strings of numbers and characters filled the screen in front of him, but he shook his head. "Nothing at all."

Battle turned his attention to Tony. The psychologist wished with all his heart that he might receive a sudden insight into the case. An impossible revelation that would save the day. But no such thought came into his head. All he could do was say, "Sorry, boss."

"Right, I'm going out there," the DCI said. "I

want to know the instant something appears on that screen. Constant radio contact."

"Got it," Toombs said. He opened a window on his computer and a list of team members' names appeared on a list. The technician selected *DCI Battle* and clicked it. He pressed a key on the keyboard and said, "Testing."

The DCI's radio crackled on his belt and Toombs' voice came through loud and clear. "Testing."

"All right," Battle said. "Keep in touch." He left them to it and marched across the IT floor to the exit.

"You can speak to any radio from here?" Tony asked, pulling his chair over next to the technician's."

"Of course," said Toombs. "Murder Force uses a bespoke system that was set up by me. As well as speaking to Battle, we can monitor what's happening." He typed a few commands and radio chatter came through the speakers.

"Dispatch to Car 45. Are you at the location yet?"
"Car 45. Arriving now."
"This is Car 36. Making approach to Lineham Road."
"Received, Car 36. Lineham Road."

Battle's voice came out of the speakers. "Toombs, do you read me?"

"Loud and clear," Toombs said.

Tony checked the timer. It had almost reached fifteen minutes. Somewhere in the city, a camera was probably being set up right now and soon, he'd see a live feed from that camera. He didn't want to. He didn't want to see someone die. He'd seen bad things before; enough to give him a lifetime's worth of nightmares.

All he could do now was wait for the timer to reach zero. It was obvious from the radio chatter that there was to be no last-minute apprehension of a suspect, no officer being in the right place at the right time. Their luck was dwindling with each second that the timer ticked off.

He got out of the chair and paced the office, expending nervous energy. He went to the window and looked up at the sky, needing to look at anything other than what was about to appear on that website, even though he knew he had to face the horror there.

He had to do it for Luke, Wendy, Laura, and Dylan Thompson.

He had to do it for the family that would appear on that screen in a few minutes.

Tony took three deep breaths and went back to his seat. He stared at the timer.

0:03.43

Battle's voice came out of the speakers of Toombs' desktop computer, cutting through the chatter. "Toombs, talk to me."

"Three minutes," the technician said. He sounded calm. Much calmer than Tony felt. Maybe he just hid his emotions well.

"All units standby," Battle said.

"The call will be made before the timer hits

zero," Toombs said to Tony. "He'll want the police to be on their way to the address before the broadcast starts."

"Are you sure?"

"That's what he did last time. The police arrived right after the feed started."

Sure enough, the female dispatcher's voice said, "Anonymous call received. Family in danger at 28 Scott Street."

"All units proceed to location," Battle said. "Do not make entry. Repeat. Do not make entry."

"The bomb squad will check the door first this time," Toombs said. "If all goes well, we might avoid a catastrophe."

Tony somehow doubted it. Wouldn't the perpetrator know they'd check for bombs this time?

The timer reached *0.00.00*

The square titled *Family Tea Party* showed grey static. Toombs clicked it and it expanded to fill the screen.

Tony gripped the arms of his chair tightly.

The static flickered and then resolved into a black-and-white image. Four people sat on a bed. They were bound, with their backs to each other. The view counter read, *15,342*. Even more people were watching this time.

"We have four people tied up on a bed," Toombs said into the microphone. "A dark-haired male, blonde female, dark-haired boy of approximately eleven or twelve years, and a blonde girl of seven or eight."

Just like the Thompsons, Tony thought. The children's ages slightly differed, but the make up of this family was identical to the Thompsons. Dark-haired father and older brother, blonde mother and younger sister.

The perpetrator had a type. These families were meant to represent a real family in his life. Perhaps his own.

"What's happening?" Battle shouted down the radio.

"Nothing," Toombs said. "They're sitting calmly on the bed. Looks like the parents' bedroom judging by the double bed and plain wallpaper. "Suggest you try that room first when you get inside."

Tony looked for wires. He didn't see any, but the camera only showed the top of the bed, not the floor. For all he knew, the room could be wired to blow as soon as someone opened the front door.

"Why aren't they moving?" he said, half to himself. The four people on the bed were alive—he could see fear in their eyes and see them breathing—but they weren't moving.

"They're tied up," Toombs said. "They can't move."

"Why aren't they moving their heads? Or speaking to each other? A parent's natural response to a high stress situation like this is to speak to their children, reassure them that everything's going to be all right. They're just staring at the walls."

CHAPTER FOUR   37

He noticed a teapot and four cups on the bedside table. Had the family been drugged?

"This is car 35. I am at location of family in danger."

"Car 35, stay in your vehicle," Battle said. "Repeat: stay in your vehicle. Stay out of the way of the bomb squad."

"This is Unit 11. We are approaching target location now."

Toombs looked at Tony and said, "Unit 11 is the bomb squad. They'll defuse any devices they find, and the family will be safe."

Tony wasn't so sure. Something didn't feel right.

"I'm at the location," Battle said. "Unit 11, let me know as soon as it's safe to make entry."

"Roger that."

"Toombs." It was Battle again. "Status report."

"They're still on the bed," the technician said. "No change."

"Checking front door for incendiary devices," said a calm voice.

Tony saw something on the video feed that made him lean closer for a better look. The children had stiffened and were frothing at the mouth. As he watched, the parents also became rigid, and saliva leaked onto their chins.

"They've been poisoned!" he shouted at Toombs. "Get the paramedics in there now!"

Toombs looked over at the video feed. All four members of the family were shaking violently. Their eyes had rolled up into their heads so that only the whites showed.

The technician leaned over the microphone. "The family has been poisoned. They need urgent medical attention."

"Unit 11," Battle snarled. 'Is the front door clear?"

"Still checking," said the calm voice.

"We need to get inside now!" Tony heard him say to someone, "Get a ladder up to that window.," and then the radio cut out.

On the screen, the parents and children were now slumped on the bed. Their restraints held them upright, but their bodies had gone limp, and their heads had dropped forward.

Shards of glass skittered onto the bed and two male paramedics entered the frame. They checked the four people on the bed, lifting their heads and shining torchlight into their eyes. They checked for pulses and then looked at each other and shook their heads.

"They're too late." Tony said.

"They spent too long checking the door," Toombs said. "If they'd gone inside sooner..." He let his words trail away.

"No," Tony said. "Those couple of minutes wouldn't have made any difference. They had no idea what poison was in their system. By the time they'd rushed them to hospital, they'd be dead on arrival. You saw how quickly they died. He set it up so there was no way we could have saved them."

"But the people watching the video won't see it like that," said Toombs.

The live feed cut off.

Tony shook his head. "They'll think the police took too long to get there and the family died as a result."

Battle's voice came over the radio. He sounded weary. Defeated. "Get the SOCOs in here. All we can do now is look for any evidence the bastard left behind."

Another voice said, *"This is DC Lines. I've been told by one of the neighbours that the family name is Goddard. There are three children. Just confirming this, as the report from the paramedics said only two children had been found. Was the third found in another part of the property? Over."*

There was some chatter as details were verified. Tony tuned it out and went over to the window, trying to get the image of the Goddard family dying out of his head.

He turned away from the view outside when Battle's voice cut through the chatter, sounding urgent. "All units. We have a missing person. David Goddard, age 12. He should have been with his family but isn't in the house. Find him."

CHAPTER
FIVE

Headquarters was buzzing with chatter when Dani got back. The search for David Goddard had begun as soon as Battle's orders had been given over the radio.

House to house enquiries were being conducted and a media campaign was underway. The twelve-year-old boy's photo was being shown on every television channel and appeals for witnesses were going out over the radio.

Tony was at his desk, scribbling in his notebook. He looked up and smiled thinly. "That didn't go well."

She dropped wearily into her seat. "Anything more on the website?"

The psychologist shook his head. "It's quiet for the moment. Toombs is keeping an eye on it."

"Why would he take a hostage, Tony?" Her greatest fear was that David Goddard was going to be the subject of the next twisted video posted on the website.

"I've been thinking about that as well," he said. "I think I know the answer, but it doesn't tell us what's going to happen to David."

"All right, what are you thinking?"

"The families are chosen because of their aesthetic. A blonde mother and daughter, and dark-haired father and son. The Thompsons were perfect, but the Goddards had an extra child, so David had to be removed for the family to fit the aesthetic."

Dani frowned. It sounded far-fetched to her, but she'd come to learn to trust Tony's instincts. "So where is David now?"

"I don't know."

"Is he still alive?"

Tony shrugged. "I don't know that either."

"This aesthetic as you call it; why is he doing that? Are the Thompsons and Goddards supposed to represent his own family, or something?"

"Most likely. They certainly represent a family he knows and has deep feelings about."

"So, he wants to kill his own family, but instead, he's killing others."

"A lot of killers find lookalikes of the people they really feel anger toward. Killing proxies can satisfy their urges for a while."

"And now he's got a twelve-year-old boy in his clutches. This isn't good, Tony."

"I know. It isn't good at all."

"Summers! Sheridan!" Battle had come in

through the door and was striding across the floor to his office.

Dani and Tony followed.

"Close the door," the DCI said as he perched on the edge of his desk.

Dani closed the door. She and Tony stood before Battle, who looked weary.

"I want you two to go home and get a good night's sleep, if you can. I need you to be fresh and alert tomorrow."

The idea of going home didn't sit well with Dani. "What about David Goddard?"

"We've got people looking for him."

"We can help."

"You won't be helping anyone if you run yourselves into the ground. I've divided the team into shifts. We're going to work around the clock on this. Don't worry, the search will go on without you.

And when you get back here tomorrow, you'll have a fresh outlook. The bloke we're after is clever. We need to have our wits about us if we're going to have any hope of catching him."

"Will you be going home as well, boss?" Tony asked.

Dani cringed inwardly. The DCI looked like he needed a good sleep, but he didn't like to be reminded of such things.

Instead of exploding, as Dani had expected, Battle simply said, "Don't worry about me. Now, get going, both of you."

CHAPTER FIVE 43

They left the office and went back to their desks. "You were pushing it a bit in there," Dani told Tony.

"He needs to be just as mentally alert as the rest of us."

"He knows that," she said.

"Does he? Because he looks like he hasn't slept in days."

"It isn't our job to look after him. He told us to go home, so that's what we do."

"Sure," Tony said. "But do you really think we'll get a great night's sleep tonight and be back here in the morning bright-eyed and bushy-tailed?"

Dani didn't answer. She knew sleep wouldn't come easily tonight. Not with a twelve-year-old kid out there somewhere. If Battle hadn't ordered her to leave, she'd have been here all night, burning the midnight oil with everyone else on the night shift.

Instead, she picked up her coat and bag and said, "Come on, we'd better get out of here before Battle has us thrown out."

Tony picked up his notebook and followed her out. As they went down the stairs, they met Ian Radcliffe on his way up.

"Going home already?" he said with a grin. He might have meant it as a joke, but Dani was in no mood for humour. She shot a grimace at the Counter Terrorism officer and stepped past him.

When they got outside the building, Tony said, "What do you think about Radcliffe?"

"I don't think anything about him. Should I?"

Tony looked back at the building, a thoughtful

look crossing his face. "I'd say we've determined that this case has nothing to do with terrorism, but he's still here. Why is he hanging around?"

"If Battle didn't want him here, he'd tell him to sling his hook," she said.

"Would he, though? I don't think Battle knows what day it is at the moment."

"That's the boss you're talking about."

"I just mean that in all the chaos, Radcliffe could be hanging around unnoticed."

Dani frowned at the psychologist. She wasn't sure what he was getting at.

"All I'm saying is we need to be wary of him," Tony said. "Something about him seems a bit off."

"He's a new face. You tend not to trust people when you first meet them."

"It isn't that. I have an instinct for these things."

She knew he was referring to the time he recognised the Lake Erie Ripper in Canada, but this situation wasn't comparable. Ian Radcliffe wasn't a serial killer Tony had been studying; he was a police officer the psychologist had only just met.

"Are you sure this isn't something to do with Ryan?" she said.

His brow furrowed. "What's that supposed to mean?"

"He wasn't who we thought he was. Maybe that's made you distrustful of people. Well, *more* distrustful, anyway."

He narrowed his eyes and raised an eyebrow. "Are you trying to psychoanalyse me?"

"I would never do that," she said innocently.

He grinned. "Maybe it's you I shouldn't trust. Trying to steal my job."

Dani laughed. "See you in the morning."

"All right," he said, taking his car keys from his pocket. "Bright-eyed and bushy-tailed, remember."

She went to her Land Rover and got in behind the wheel. She turned the radio on and heard Gallow's voice coming from the speakers. The Superintendent was talking to the press, telling them the bare minimum and trying to ensure the public that they were in no danger. He added a caveat to that last part, telling everyone to stay vigilant and look out for their neighbours.

Dani listened to the press conference during the drive home. Most of the questions from the reporters were about David Goddard. Were the police hopeful that they'd find the boy alive? Was there any evidence to suggest that David had poisoned his family and run away?

Gallow assured them that the police hoped to find David alive. Regarding the suggestion that the boy might have poisoned his family, the superintendent said that only the gutter press would ask such a thing. David was just as much a victim as the other members of his family.

By the time Dani got home, a debate was raging on the radio about whether the police force should have high profile departments like Murder Force or if their existence might cause publicity seekers to commit crimes just to get on the telly.

She got out of the Land Rover and looked out over the North Yorkshire Moors. No matter how bad her day had been, seeing the moors always calmed her.

As she approached the front door of her cottage, she heard Barney and Jack—her German shepherds—scrabbling at the other side of the door and whining in anticipation of her arrival.

Both dogs ran out when she opened the door and circled her, wagging tails beating against her legs.

"All right, you two, let's get inside," she said, ruffling the fur on the backs of their necks. "We'll have something to eat first, and then go for a walk. How does that sound?"

Barney and Jack followed her inside, staying close to her legs. She filled their bowls with food and opened the fridge in search of something for herself.

She checked the shelf she reserved for ready meals, found a lasagna, and tossed it into the microwave.

While that was heating up, and the dogs were still eating, she went to her bedroom, stripped, and had a quick shower. The microwave was beeping when she got out.

Donning her robe, she returned to the kitchen and took the lasagna out, sliding the hot plastic container onto a plate and placing it onto the kitchen counter.

While the food cooled, she went back to the

bedroom and put on an old pair of jeans and a dark green knitted jumper.

The dogs had finished eating now, and were waiting for her by the front door, tails thumping on the floor.

"Let me eat my tea," she told them. "Then we'll go for a nice, long walk."

She needed to get out in the fresh air to clear her head. A long walk over the moors with Barney and Jack was the best self-care routine she knew, and the dogs loved it.

She ate the lasagna quickly and put her hiking boots on. The dogs, sensing what was coming, wheeled around crazily near the wall hook from which their leads hung.

Dani attached the leads to the dogs' collars and took Barney and Jack outside and across the road to the moors.

Once there, she released them and trudged over the grass and heather as they ran all over the place, following her in a haphazard fashion that involved returning to her side every few minutes before dashing off again and chasing each other in circles.

Dani breathed in the fresh, cool air and tried to take her mind off the case. It was difficult, especially with David Goddard missing, but she reminded herself that her colleagues were out there looking for him. There was nothing more she could do until she was back on duty tomorrow. And by then, David might even have been found.

The question Gallow had been asked on the radio came back to her.

Do the police hope to find the boy alive? Or are you looking for a—

Gallow had interrupted before the reporter had said, "body," and assured everyone at the press conference, and everyone listening, that the police were indeed hoping to find David Goddard alive.

What we wish for and what we get are two different things, Dani's mother used to say to her when she was a child. She hoped the sentiment wasn't proved true where David Goddard was concerned.

She kept wondering why the man who poisoned the Goddards would take David from the house and not leave him to suffer the same fate as the rest of his family. Such things were more in Tony's purview than her own, but it bothered her, nevertheless.

She forced herself to stop thinking about it, especially when her mind went to some dark places, and concentrated instead on the dogs and the moors.

She got home almost two hours later, returning to a dark house. She switched the lights on and built a fire in the fireplace, which the dogs immediately lay in front of. They were exhausted, and so was Dani.

She poured herself a glass of wine and sat in front of the window, watching as darkness crept across the landscape.

If David was still alive—and she had to believe that he was—he would probably be feeling even more afraid as the night drew in. She wondered if he knew what had happened to his parents and siblings.

As the moors became lost to darkness, she whispered a silent prayer. "Please let him be alive."

CHAPTER
SIX

When Tony got back to his flat, Alina was in the kitchen, making spaghetti bolognese. He'd rung her and told her he was on his way, and it looked like she'd jumped into action immediately. She was stirring the spaghetti in one pan while making the sauce in another.

The kitchen smelled of basil, tomatoes, onions, and oregano, making Tony's mouth water.

"Something smells good," he said, dropping his notebook on the counter. He leaned down and kissed Alina.

"What's good is you being back at a reasonable hour," she said, giving the sauce another stir before transferring a tray of garlic bread from the counter to the oven.

"Battle sent us home. Well, some of us. He's got the Force working round the clock in shifts."

"I heard about the missing boy. That's terrible, Tony. I can't imagine how scared he is." She looked genuinely upset and that was one of the things Tony loved about her; she was always sympathetic to other people's plights. She had a big heart, which sometimes surprised him, especially considering she worked in a field which often hardened people's emotions.

"I'm sure we'll find him," he said, to reassure her if nothing else. On his way home, he'd heard Gallow tell the press they expected to find David Goddard alive, but he knew that was simply to keep the media happy. Gallow knew as well as anyone else that the chances of finding anything other than David's body were slim.

"I hope so," Alina said.

"So do I." Despite his fear that David was already dead, he hoped with all his heart that the boy would be found safe and well, even if experience told him that was an unlikely outcome.

"I don't understand why he would take a child." Alina was stirring the sauce again, adding a pinch of salt and fresh, chopped basil.

"Children are taken all the time," Tony said.

"Yes, but this person isn't like that, is he? It seems to me he has a grudge against the police. He's killed four children already. He didn't take them. So why is David different?"

"I don't know yet. It's probably because David was simply an inconvenience. This guy seems to be targeting families that consist of two children. The Goddards had three, so the math was wrong. David was simply surplus to requirements."

"Tony, that's a horrible thing to say! He is a child. A living, human being."

"I'm only telling you how our killer thinks. At least, I'm fairly sure that's how he thinks. I don't know yet." He felt suddenly weary. It had been a long day and the deaths he'd witnessed were affecting him even more than he'd anticipated. It seemed like every time he closed his eyes, he saw the Goddard family choking on poison.

"Are you okay, Tony?" Alina touched his shoulder gently and looked into his eyes as if assessing his mental state. "You don't look okay."

"It's been a long day," he said.

"Sit down," she said. "Dinner won't be long."

"I think I'll have a shower first and get changed."

"Of course. Are you sure you're okay?"

He nodded. "I'll be fine. There's a bottle of red somewhere. Why don't you open it and let it breathe?"

He went into the bathroom and ran the shower, dialling the temperature up as hot as he could stand it. Undressing quickly and getting in, he gasped when the spray hit him like a thousand hot needles against his skin. When he was sure he couldn't stand it any longer, he turned the dial to cold.

He let out a breath as the suddenly-cold water hit his skin and made him shiver.

This was a technique he'd learned long ago to bring his thoughts into the present moment. It didn't cleanse the other stuff from his mind, but it helped him focus on the here and now for a while.

He turned off the water and dried himself quickly before padding naked to the bedroom and putting on a pair of jeans and a black T-shirt that had the logo of a motorbike company on the front. He wasn't sure why he'd bought it; he didn't even know how to ride a motorbike.

Alina was dishing out the pasta when he returned to the kitchen.

"Feeling better?" she asked.

"Yes," he said, realising that he *did* feel a bit better. "More refreshed."

"Good. Now, sit down and I will pour the wine."

He took a seat and looked at the dish in front of him. The smells coming from his plate were amazing.

"One day, I will make you *sarmale* and *mămăligă*," she said, pouring the wine and sitting down at the table with him.

"I'd really like that," he said, pushing his fork into the spaghetti on his plate and twisting it. "I have absolutely no idea what those are, but I'm assuming they're Romanian."

She grinned. "Yes, they're Romanian. My mother taught me how to make them and I have a secret family recipe."

"Well, if they're anything like this bolognese, I can't wait. It's delicious."

"Thank you. I'm just glad we get to share it together. I must thank Stewart sometime, for sending you home for the evening. How is he, anyway? I have not seen him for a while."

"As cranky as ever."

She raised an eyebrow. "I never found him to be that way."

"You only had to deal with him at the morgue. You weren't taking direct orders from him."

"I am sure he is not that bad."

"No, I suppose not. He's just passionate about his job and sometimes that comes out as anger directed at those around him."

"You have psychoanalysed him?"

"Of course. I psychoanalyse everyone. It's a habit."

"Even me?"

He smiled. "Especially you."

"And what have you learned?"

"That you're a wonderful cook."

"That is not what I meant. You're not playing fair."

"Playing? So that's all my job is to you? A game?" He tried to look offended but couldn't pull it off because he was laughing too much.

"Now you're twisting my words." She made a pouting expression that was greatly exaggerated and that made him laugh even more.

"All right," he said, relenting, "I'll tell you what I've learned from psychoanalysing you. You're a beautiful person, both inside and out."

"No, tell me something real."

"That is real."

"Something bad."

"Bad?"

"We all have psychological issues, don't we? What is one of mine?"

He had to think hard to find one. Alina really was one of the most balanced people he'd ever come across.

"Come on, Tony. There must be something."

"All right. You have a preoccupation with death."

"I'm an anthropologist. I'm supposed to have a preoccupation with death."

"True, but you seem fascinated with it, sometimes. And not just in a work context. Yesterday, we walked past a dead pigeon on the pavement, and you stopped to have a good look at it."

"The dead can tell us so much about how they lived. You're right. I *am* fascinated."

"In a pigeon?"

"Just because it is a pigeon does not mean it isn't worthy of our attention. This particular pigeon had a scar on its right leg, maybe from a fight with another pigeon some time ago. It was missing a toe on its left foot, probably because there was a hairdresser's shop across the road. And it was killed by a cat, if you're interested."

"Wait a minute. Hairdresser? What's that got to do with a pigeon's missing toe?" He spun his fork through the spaghetti and slid the captured strands through the rich sauce before pushing them into his mouth.

"A study was done in Paris," she said, "and it was discovered that the more hairdressers there are in an area, the more missing toes the pigeons in the area will have."

Tony frowned in confusion. "I don't see the correlation."

"Strands of hair escape from the shop into the environment. Some of them get wrapped around pigeons' toes and cut off the circulation. The toes eventually fall off."

Tony took a sip of wine. "You know too many weird things."

"The dead can tell us their stories, Tony. They are not weird; they are interesting. That pigeon lived a full life just outside this window and we did not know anything about it until it died and told us of its life. That is beautiful."

He'd never looked at it like that before. Alina had a different way of seeing things that made him re-evaluate his own thought patterns. Was he too stuck in his ways? He didn't see beauty in dead pigeons or dead people. He just saw death.

An image came unbidden into his mind's eye. It was one he often remembered without meaning to and he wished he could forget it.

"Tony, what are you thinking?" Alina looked concerned.

"Nothing." He wished it *was* nothing.

"No, it is not nothing. I have seen that expression before. You are thinking of *him*, aren't you?"

"Who?"

"The Lake Erie Ripper."

He decided to come clean. He didn't want to lie

to her. "I was remembering the moment I slipped into his house. What I saw there."

"You should not think of such things if they upset you."

"Those girls," he said. In his mind, he was no longer in his kitchen in York. He was entering a house in a small town called Lakeshore near Lake St. Clair in Canada. "Their bodies told stories too. But they were ugly stories that ended in tragedy."

She got up and came around the table to him, stroking his forehead as he stared down at the plate of spaghetti in front of him.

"Tony, you must not dwell on such things. It is merely a single moment among millions. You must put it in its proper place. It belongs in the past."

"I know. But sometimes, it's hard to forget. And when things happen…like today…it brings it all back."

"If you must think of that moment. don't dwell on the girls you couldn't help," she said softly. "Remember the two girls you rescued from that house. If not for you, they would not be alive today."

He knew that, but it didn't help him see past the horror that was within that house.

"Come on," Alina said. "Let's finish our meal, then go for a walk. It's a lovely evening."

"All right," he said, "but if we see a dead pigeon, I'm going to keep walking. You can catch up with me when you've finished examining it."

She smiled and nodded. "Deal."

Later, long after the midnight hour had passed, Tony got out of bed and padded over to the window. He'd managed to get some sleep, but he'd been woken three times by nightmares.

The first had been a graphic mental tour of the Lake Erie Ripper's house. Nothing new there. He had that nightmare often.

In the second, he'd been standing in the Goddard family's bedroom while the poison had taken effect. He'd watched them die all over again.

And in the third nightmare—the one that had woken him less than a minute ago—he'd been in the Ripper's house again. Only this time, there was a voice calling out for help. A young boy's voice. Tony had searched the dream house from top to bottom, but the boy was nowhere to be found. The disembodied voice had continued to cry out for help until Tony had woken up.

The city of York slept and was mostly dark except for the glowing streetlights and an occasional car headlight on a distant street.

"Tony, come back to bed." Alina's voice was sleepy.

He took a final look at the night before slipping back under the covers.

She put her arm over his chest and nestled her face against his shoulder. "Couldn't sleep?"

"Not really. Nightmares."

"Don't worry, Tony, you'll find him."

"Find who?"

"The missing boy."

She knew him too well. He turned to face her and kissed her forehead.

"Now get some sleep," she said. "You won't be able to help anyone if you're tired."

He turned on his side so he could see the night sky through the window. He'd had nights like this before and knew he wouldn't be able to get back to sleep.

But as he listened to Alina breathing next to him and watched the stars, his eyelids grew heavy, and he let himself drift into a sleep that was devoid of nightmares. No more houses or ghostly voices.

Just restful sleep.

CHAPTER
SEVEN

Scarborough

Frank Moseley sauntered along the South Bay promenade at midnight. He needed to find somewhere to bed down for the night. Once the dawn came, he'd be moved on by the police, so he had to get a few hours of shuteye in before then.

Beyond the railing, the beach was pitch black. The illumination from the streetlights that lit the promenade spilled onto the sand, but died after a few feet, swallowed by the inky blackness.

Frank didn't like the beach. Not anymore. He used to sleep on the sand sometimes, but something bad happened two years ago, and he never went there at night anymore. Even though he had a dog now, he feared the beach.

What he needed was a nice shop doorway.

"Don't worry, boy," he said to Lucky. "We'll soon have a bed for the night."

Upon hearing his name, Lucky glanced up at Frank briefly before returning his attention to the way ahead.

The dog was Frank's only companion. He'd found Lucky in an alley behind a fish and chip shop. The animal had taken an instant liking to Frank. That had been a year ago, and they'd become, and remained, best friends ever since.

In fact, Lucky was Frank's only friend. Some time ago—he wasn't exactly sure when because thinking about it made his brain muddled—Frank had lived what some people might call an *ordinary* life. He'd had a job, and a wife, and friends. But when his wife had died, Frank had abandoned his old life. He'd left everything—including his friends and everything else that reminded him of his former life—behind.

Now, he only had the dog. And he was fine with that.

He heard a vehicle driving along the road behind him and didn't take much notice of it until it slowed down, matching his pace. Frank side-eyed it. A black van. He couldn't see the driver.

Lucky turned his head to stare at the vehicle as he trotted along the promenade.

"Never mind that, boy," Frank said. "It's nothing to do with us."

The van's window buzzed down, and a voice said, "Frank Moseley?"

That took Frank aback. He'd been approached by vehicles before. Sometimes, the driver wanted to hurl insults at him, telling him he was ruining the town. Sometimes, they wanted something else. Frank ignored them either way.

But no one had ever known his name. As far as they knew, he was nameless and homeless. So how did the van driver know who he was?

Was it one of his old friends? The ones he'd left behind in that life that seemed so distant he could hardly believe it was he who'd lived it?

He stopped in his tracks. The van stopped too.

"Who are you?" Frank said to the driver, whose face was hidden by shadows.

"You don't know me. I saw you in the papers."

"The papers?" The only time he'd been in the papers was when he'd been recovering in hospital after the event on the beach.

"Yes. You were in a hospital bed after being rescued by that retired copper. I saw your photo. That was you, wasn't it?"

Frank nodded hesitantly. Was this man a reporter come to do a follow up story, or something? "Yeah, that was me."

"Get in. I'd like to talk to you."

Frank took a step backwards. "No, thanks." He had a rule: don't get in people's cars. And he wasn't about to break it just because this feller knew his name.

The passenger door opened, but the van's interior light didn't come on. The driver remained in darkness. One thing Frank could see clearly, though, was the gun the man held. A gun pointing straight at him.

"Get in," the driver repeated, more firmly this time.

Frank weighed up his options and realised he didn't have any. There was nobody around at this late hour. Nobody he could call out to for help. And even if there was, they'd just ignore him. One thing he'd learned quickly when living on the streets was that he, and people like him, were ignored by everyone else. It was as if they existed in a different world that "regular" people couldn't glimpse into.

"All right," he said, "I'll get in." Then, a sudden panic gripped him, and he said, "Please don't hurt my dog."

"I'm not going to hurt the dog."

Frank breathed a sigh of relief. "Come on, Lucky. This man won't hurt you."

"The dog stays here."

"But he won't know where I've gone. *I* don't know where I'm going."

"Don't worry about that. If you don't want the dog to get hurt, leave it here."

Frank crouched down and ran his hands through Lucky's rough fur. "Don't worry, boy. I'll be back soon. I'll find you again."

He climbed into the van. Lucky went to follow, but Frank pushed him back. "You stay here, boy."

Lucky whimpered.

"Close the door," the driver said. Frank could see

his face now, illuminated by the streetlights through the windscreen. He was younger than Frank had expected, perhaps in his mid-twenties. A scar ran from his hairline to his eyebrow.

"I think Lucky will wait for me here," Frank said, to reassure himself.

"You don't need to worry about that dog anymore," the driver said, pulling away from the kerb. "Soon, you won't have to worry about anything anymore."

Leaving the dog alone on the promenade, the van disappeared into the night.

CHAPTER
EIGHT

The next morning, Dani arrived at work to find Battle on the warpath. The night shift hadn't made any headway in the search for David Goddard and the DCI was storming around headquarters looking for someone to blame.

Superintendent Gallow had returned from his trip to Scotland, which might also account for some of Battle's dark mood. The two had exchanged a few words behind closed doors and that event had directly preceded Battle's anger.

Dani kept her head down. Best to go unnoticed and not draw the DCI's ire.

"Morning," Tony said, arriving through the door. He tossed his notebook onto his desk. "Any news?" He sat in his chair and looked at her expectantly.

"I don't think things went well last night," she said, nodding towards Battle, who was now in his office with the door shut, shouting at someone down the telephone.

"Doesn't look good," Tony said.

Dani's desk phone rang. She answered it and heard Chris Toombs' voice.

"I just tried to talk to Battle," he said, "and he chewed me out for not getting results. He didn't give me a chance to tell him why I was ringing."

"He's not in the best of moods," Dani told him.

"Well, his loss is your gain. I think I've managed to track down the owner of the website."

"Who is it?"

"I haven't clicked the button yet. I found a back door into the code. I was going to do a big live reveal for Battle, but since he's indisposed, I can do it for you, if you like."

"I didn't realise you were so dramatic, Toombs."

"I prefer to call myself a showman."

"I'll be there in a minute. I'll bring Tony."

"Great. The more, the merrier."

"What's up?" Tony said when she put the phone down.

"Toombs may have found who owns the website."

"Who is it?"

"Don't know yet. He wants us to be there when he clicks the button."

"Right, let's go."

They went down to IT and found Toombs in his office. His computer screen was filled with computer code.

"Ready for the reveal?" he asked as they entered.

"I hope this isn't anticlimactic," Tony said.

"It shouldn't be. I found a back door into the site's code. That led me to a bunch of IP metadata which means I can see the site owner's name and address."

"All right," said Dani, "Press the button, or whatever you do."

"Very well." Toombs cracked his knuckles. "I can now tell you that the person who owns this site is…" He positioned his finger over the keyboard and dropped it dramatically, entering a line of code. He leaned towards the screen and said, "Gregory Marlon Hughes."

When she heard the name, Dani felt a shock go through her body. That couldn't be right. She must have misheard.

"And he lives at…" Toombs said.

"Flanders Road, Scarborough," Dani finished for him.

Both Toombs and Tony looked at her.

"That's spot on," Toombs said. "How did you—"

"Greg Hughes was my first partner when I joined the force. He was my mentor. He trained me. When you said the name, I thought it must be another Greg Hughes, but his middle name was Marlon, after his grandfather. He told me one day when we were talking about television programmes."

She still couldn't believe that Greg Hughes—the Greg Hughes she knew and had worked with all those years ago—was involved with these crimes. It didn't seem possible. Greg had been a gentle, kind man. It was inconceivable that he would do something like this.

"Just a minute," Toombs said. His fingers flew over the keyboard. "There's an ID attached to his account. I should be able to bring it up."

An image appeared on the screen. It was Greg's driving licence, and now there was no doubt that this was the man who had taken Dani under his wing when she'd joined the police force.

In the photo on the licence, he looked older than she remembered, but there was no doubt it was the same man.

"When did you last see Hughes?" Tony asked.

"He retired years ago. I haven't heard from him since then."

She felt suddenly guilty for not keeping in touch with Greg. It was too easy to lose track of people over time. She'd somehow let one of the most important relationships of her career fade away into nothing more than a memory.

"Is he capable of something like this?" Tony said, pointing at the laptop with the *Will the police save them?* site on its screen.

"No." She shook her head, as if to convince herself. "He didn't know anything about computers. Greg was old school; he'd take paper and pen over a keyboard any day."

"Could he have developed some sort of grudge against the police since he retired?"

"No. Why would he? He loved his job, loved

helping people. I'm telling you, there's some kind of mistake."

"I guess we'll find out when we have a word with him."

"We should run this past Battle first," she said. "He'll want to know."

Leaving Toombs in his office, they went back upstairs. Battle was in his office. The door was closed.

Dani knocked gingerly on it.

The DCI looked up and nodded. "Come in, Summers."

She and Tony entered and closed the door behind them.

"What is it?" Battle said gruffly.

"Is everything all right, guv?"

"No, everything isn't all right. There's no word on the Goddard boy and I've been informed that Tom Ryan is coming back today."

"That's good news, isn't it?" Tony said. "An extra pair of hands to help with the search."

"You think it's good, do you?" the DCI said. "You think it's good that we've got to pretend he's a copper while he's actually reporting to MI-bloody-5. That he's going to be lying to our co-workers out there and there's nothing we can do about it?"

Tony looked uncomfortable. "Since you put it like that…" He didn't finish the sentence.

"What have you two got for me? I'm sure you didn't come in here just to talk about spies and double agents."

"Toombs got a hit on the website owner," Tony said.

"Well, that's good news. Bring them in and question them. Our priority is to find out what they've done with David Goddard. Summers, you can be lead interviewer."

"It isn't as simple as that, guv," she said.

The DCI frowned at her. "What do you mean?"

"The person is an old partner of mine. A retired copper."

He raised an eyebrow. "Ex-copper with a grudge, is it? This won't look good to the public."

"I don't think it's him," Dani said. "There's no way he did any of this. When I knew him, he was a kind, gentle man."

"When you knew him, he may have been," Battle said. "People change. Bring him in. If he owns the website, then he's involved in some way and he's the only lead we've got. Is he local?"

"He lives in Scarborough, guv."

"Right. Get over to his house and nick him. I'll get dispatch to send a couple of uniforms as back up, but we'll keep it low key. We don't need a media circus."

"Got it, guv."

"Can I go as well?" Tony asked.

Battle looked at him, pursing his lips and furrowing his brow. After a moment's consideration, he said, "All right. Perhaps you can talk him into revealing the location of the boy."

"I'll try."

"I'll sort out a search warrant for the address," the DCI said. "Get going."

They left the DCI's office and Dani got her bag from her desk, trying to come to terms with the fact that she was about to arrest Greg Hughes. The man had been like a father to her at one time and now she was going to put him in cuffs.

Tony didn't seem to have any such qualms. He'd arrived in a good mood and now seemed even happier as they descended the stairs to the car park.

"You're in a good mood," she said to him.

"We're one step closer to finding David Goddard. If Hughes decides to come clean and confess, we could have David safely in our custody by lunchtime."

"You think he's still alive?"

"I don't know. I have to believe he could be."

She remembered her whispered prayer at the window last night. She wasn't one for religion, or any kind of spiritual belief, but she'd be happy to have that prayer answered.

They got into her Land Rover. While Tony put his seatbelt on, Dani started the engine and tried to mentally steel herself for what she was about to do. Was it possible that Greg Hughes had orchestrated the deaths of the Thompson and Goddard families?

She just couldn't believe it.

As they drove towards the coast from the city, Tony was unusually quiet. He looked out of the window as the landscape rolled by and said nothing.

"Penny for 'em," Dani said. Tony might be experiencing some sort of zen calmness, but her own mind was in turmoil, and she needed a conversation that would distract her from her thoughts about Greg.

Tony turned to face her. "I wasn't really thinking about much, to be honest. Just replaying last night in my head."

"Okay, perhaps I don't want to know, after all."

"No, nothing like that. Alina made spaghetti and then we went for a walk. It was nice."

"I'm pleased for you. You two seem to really hit it off."

He grinned. "Yeah, we do."

She remembered her own evening. Walking the dogs had been fun, and she loved to see them expending their energy on the moors, but might it have been more enjoyable if someone else had been there with her?

She pushed the thought away. When Shaun died, she'd told herself there wouldn't be anyone else, despite promising her husband only days before his death that she'd move on with her life.

Well, she had moved on, hadn't she? She was now a member of an elite, high-profile police team. Shaun couldn't say she hadn't done what she'd promised.

Except, she knew he hadn't meant her to move on only in her career; he'd wanted her to find someone else to share the rest of her life with.

She usually kept such thoughts bottled up, but

sitting next to loved-up Tony had brought them bubbling to the surface.

"How are you?" he asked, perhaps perceiving that something was on her mind.

"I'm fine." She kept her eyes on the road.

"How was your evening?"

"Great. I went on a two-hour hike with the dogs over the moors."

"Nice. How are the dogs?"

"A handful, as always."

"I bet they are. What did you have for tea?"

"A microwave lasagna."

"Quick and easy."

She could tell he was purposely keeping the conversation light. Had he guessed what she's been thinking after he mentioned his evening with Alina? He wasn't *that* perceptive, was he?

"I'm sorry about your friend," he said, after a pause.

"Friend?"

"Greg Hughes. It must be a shock."

"It's more than a shock, Tony. It's unbelievable."

"Sometimes we think we know people, but they're hiding dark secrets," he offered by way of an explanation.

"Not Greg Hughes. He's straightforward and down-to-earth. What you see is what you get with him."

"Maybe the retirement years haven't been good to him. Some coppers can't let the job go. That can affect people in different ways."

"He was looking forward to retirement. He was going to go travelling with his wife, and then they were going to potter around the house and garden together. Go the beach. Spend their days doing whatever they wanted."

She told herself that she's lost contact with Greg during the time he was travelling around the world with his wife.

That would make more sense than the alternative; that the only thing they had in common was the job and since he was no longer on the job, they had nothing to talk about.

"What if something happened to his wife and his plans went up in smoke?"

Dani shook her head. "Even if something happened to Helen, Greg wouldn't go off the rails. Not like this."

"We'll know soon, I suppose," Tony said noncommittally. "More importantly, we might find out what happened to David Goddard."

Dani bit her lip. Part of her was afraid to find out what had happened to the twelve-year-old.

When they reached Scarborough, a light rain was falling over the seaside town. A few dog walkers trudged along the beach in waterproof jackets, but the grey clouds seemed to have chased everyone else away. The town was quiet and sombre.

At least, it seemed that way to Dani, but knew she might be letting her emotions colour her view of the world at the moment.

When they reached Flanders Road, a patrol car was waiting for them on the corner. Dani brought the Land Rover up beside it and rolled down her window. The officer behind the wheel in the patrol car did the same.

"Are you my backup?" Dani asked him.

"Yes, ma'am."

"I want one of you at the front door with me, the other around the back in case he does a runner." She could hardly believe she was saying that about her old mentor and friend.

"Understood," the officer said.

Dani drove slowly along Flanders Road until she got to Greg's house, a detached three-bed that had been built in the eighties.

There was a white Fiat on the drive. She hoped that didn't mean Greg—who preferred larger cars—wasn't at home.

"You wait here," she told Tony as the patrol car parked behind her and the uniformed officers got out.

The psychologist nodded.

She got out of the Land Rover and walked to the front door with one of the officers while the other slipped around the side of the house.

After taking a deep breath, Dani knocked on the front door.

She heard movement inside. Someone approaching the door. It opened and a mousey woman in her sixties peered out. "Yes?"

"Helen?" Dani asked. She hadn't met the woman

many times, but she was sure this was Helen Hughes.

The woman nodded. "That's right. Can I help you?"

"You may not remember me—"

"Dani," Helen said, squinting at her. "I recognise you now. Of course I remember you."

"Is Greg in?"

Helen's face dropped. "Oh, that's right, you don't know, do you?"

"Know what?" Dani asked.

"Greg is dead. He died two years ago."

CHAPTER
NINE

"Dead?" Dani's legs felt suddenly weak. She'd psyched herself up for a confrontation with her old partner; she hadn't been ready to confront the news of his death.

"Come in and I'll put the kettle on," Helen said.

Dani nodded. She turned to the uniformed officer. You can return to your regular duties. Thank you.

He nodded. "Ma'am."

"Can I bring my partner in as well?" she asked Helen.

"Yes, of course. I'll get the kettle on." Helen disappeared into the house.

Dani waved at Tony. He got out of the Land Rover and came up the drive.

"I've just learned that Greg is dead," she said. "He's been dead for two years."

"What?" Tony looked confused. "Then how could he have set up that website?"

"He obviously didn't. Get hold of Toombs. Find out when the site was put up online."

He nodded and started tapping on his phone as they entered the house.

"Make yourselves at home," Helen called from the kitchen. "The living room is just to your right."

The living room was cosy, with a settee and armchair arranged around an electric fire. Photos of Helen and Greg, taken in various parts of the world, sat on the mantelpiece and hung on the walls.

Dani was pleased to see that Greg had gone on his planned worldwide adventure after retiring from the force.

"Toombs has texted me back," Tony said. "The website was set up in Greg's name a month ago."

"So, someone is using his identity."

Tony nodded. "Looks like it."

"But why Greg?"

"It could be random," Tony offered.

"It doesn't feel random."

"No, it doesn't," he admitted.

"Here we are," Helen said, coming through the door with a tray balanced in her hands. She placed it on the coffee table in front of the settee. "Help yourselves. And have a seat. No need to stand to attention."

"Thanks, Helen," Dani said, sitting on the settee while Tony poured tea for all three of them from a China pot with a floral design.

"What did you want to see Greg about?" Helen said. "You looked very serious standing on the doorstep with that uniformed officer. Is he not joining us?"

Dani was glad Helen hadn't seen the other officer stationed by the back door. "No, he has to get back to his duties. I was hoping Greg could help with a case we're working on, that's all."

Helen looked confused. "A case? After all this time? I can't see how he could have helped you, dear."

"It doesn't matter," Dani said. "How did Greg die, if you don't mind my asking?"

Helen's eyes dropped to her hands, which were clasped together in her lap. "Well, that's a bone of contention between myself and the police."

"Oh? Why's that?"

"They said it was suicide," Helen said, tears springing into her eyes. "I don't believe it. I *won't* believe it, no matter how many times they tell me. Not Greg. He wouldn't do that. He loved life."

Dani had to admit that Greg Hughes was the last person she would have thought might take his own life, but she knew that such things as depression were often hidden.

"Can you tell me what happened?" she said gently.

Helen wiped her eyes with a balled-up tissue she took from her cardigan pocket and nodded. "It was all so sudden. One minute, Greg and I were planning a holiday in the Maldives and the next, he disappeared."

She wiped her eyes again and said, "he went to

the chemist to get my Tramadol prescription. It's for my back. I've been in pain for over a decade, ever since I fell down a flight of stairs at a restaurant. Anyway, that's by the by. Greg never picked up the prescription and he never came home. He was missing for two days before they found him."

"Found him?" Dani prompted.

"His body," Helen said in a single breath that came out like a sigh. "He was on the beach. They said he drowned. I told them that wasn't possible. Greg was a good swimmer. They said he'd drowned on purpose. Drowned himself is what they meant. I didn't believe it then, and I don't believe it now. Greg would never do that. He wouldn't leave me alone."

She wiped at her eyes, but some of the tears escaped and rolled down her cheeks.

"What do you think happened to your husband, Mrs Hughes?" Tony asked softly from the armchair. He leaned forward and touched her arm gently.

"Isn't it obvious? Someone murdered him. Greg put a lot of people away during his career. Perhaps someone saw him on the street and recognised him. They probably wanted revenge."

"Did the police look into that?" Dani asked.

"No, they didn't. Once the pathologist decided Greg had drowned, that was that. They said he either fell into the sea or went in on purpose with the intention of killing himself. It doesn't make any sense, Dani."

"You said Greg was missing for two days," Dani said. "Did you find out where he'd been?"

"I have no idea. He hadn't been in the water all that time, that's for sure. He was found in the early hours of the morning and the pathologist said he'd only been in the sea a few hours before that. I don't know where he was during those two days. The police don't either."

It sounded suspicious to Dani, mostly because she knew Greg and found it difficult to believe he'd abandon Helen like that. He'd at least leave a note explaining his actions.

That was the type of person Greg had been for as long as Dani had known him. He was meticulous and hated loose ends. He wouldn't end his own life in such an enigmatic way.

"He was very proud of you, you know," Helen said. "At least he got a chance to see you just before he died."

"See me?" Dani felt confused. "I didn't see Greg just before he died, Helen."

"No, but he saw you. On telly. You were trying to find that killer who was leaving girls' bodies on the moors."

"The Snow Killer?"

Helen frowned. "I thought he was called the Red Ribbon Killer."

"He was called that as well," Dani said. She'd hated the names the media had given to the killer who'd left his victims encased in ice on the moors, but the moniker "Red Ribbon Killer" had rankled her the most of all because it had contained information she'd been trying to keep from the press: the fact that the killer had tied a red ribbon in his victims' hair before dumping their bodies.

"Well, anyway, Greg saw you on the news," Helen said. "He was very proud of the work you were doing."

Dani offered a thin-lipped smile as acknowledgement. Her mind was running over the circumstances surrounding Greg's death. Where had he been for two days? How had he ended up drowning in the sea? Why hadn't he left a note, or communicated with his wife in some way?

Tony's phone buzzed. He looked down at it and slipped it into his pocket. "Thank you for the tea, Mrs Hughes," he said, putting his empty cup back on the tray. "It was lovely. I'm afraid we've got to be going."

Dani followed his lead. "Yes, thank you, Helen. I'm so sorry for your loss. Greg was a lovely man."

"He was," Helen said. "I miss him every day."

"Of course you do." Dani took her card out of her bag and placed it on the coffee table. "If you ever want to ring me and just chat, that's my number."

"Thanks, Dani."

She saw them to the door. As Dani stepped outside, she said, "Just one more thing, Helen. Where is the chemist Greg went to for your prescription?"

"There are some shops about half a mile away," Helen said. "A mini-supermarket, a Chinese takeaway, and the chemist. They aren't far. That's why Greg walked there. Said he liked the exercise."

"Thanks." Dani got into the Land Rover with Tony and started the engine. "Who was that on the phone?"

"Toombs texted me again. He said there's been a development.

"Ring him back. I want to see exactly where this chemist is. She used her phone to locate the nearest shops and turned around at the end of the road. As she drove back along Flanders Road, Helen was still standing in the doorway of her house. She and Dani exchanged a brief wave.

"Chris, what's happening?" Tony said into his phone as Dani reached the junction that took them onto the main road.

A left turn that took them past the shops Helen had mentioned. They weren't far from the house at all. If something had happened to Greg—if he'd been abducted—then it must have happened close to home. That suggested someone had been watching him rather than a random meeting on the street.

"Right. Okay." The psychologist nodded and then put his phone back into his pocket.

"Well?" Dani asked. "What did he say?"

"Another countdown has appeared on the website. Two hours."

"Two hours? That doesn't give us much time."

"The video has a title," Tony said. "Considering what we've just been talking to Helen about, it's a bit eerie."

"What do you mean? What is it?"

Tony looked at her and said, *"Man in the water."*

CHAPTER
TEN

They arrived at headquarters just over an hour later. Dani was acutely aware of the small amount of time left before the next atrocity took place.

She and Tony rushed into the building and up the stairs to Toombs' office.

Battle was in there, standing behind the computer technician's chair. His face was set in a grim expression, and he looked tired. Dani wondered if he'd managed to get any sleep since yesterday.

"Summers, I want you with me," the DCI said. "As soon as we get an address, we're going straight over there. I've got an ambulance on standby."

"Right, guv."

"You're staying here with Toombs," he told Tony.

The psychologist looked , but he nodded. "Okay, boss."

On the laptop screen, a third square had

appeared, titled *Man in the water*. The timer above it was currently at, *0:47.33*

Less than an hour, Dani thought. *In less than an hour, someone else is going to die at the hands of this maniac.*

"Tell me about Hughes," Battle said.

"He died two years ago, guv. Whoever set up this site used his identity."

"Are they responsible for his death?"

"I think it's likely. Greg drowned, but that doesn't mean he wasn't held underwater. And the person who set this site up had Greg's driving licence. He used it as a form of ID."

"We'll look into it," the DCI said.

"Guys," Toombs said, pointing at the screen.

Another square had appeared. There was no title, but the timer exactly matched the timer above the *Man in the water* square. *0:45.57*

"What the hell's this?" Battle said, leaning forwards and narrowing his eyes at the laptop.

"He's splitting our resources," Tony said. "Two events at the same time."

Dani felt her stomach drop. They never knew what to expect. This man was one step ahead of them every time. She voiced a thought she'd had in the car on the way here.

"I think he's been planning this for years."

Battle looked at her quizzically. "Why do you think that?"

"Greg died two years ago. If this guy is responsible for that, he could have been planning this the whole time. He used Greg's ID to register the website a month ago. Everything we've seen from him is meticulously planned and orchestrated. This isn't a spur of the moment crime spree; it's the culmination of years of work."

"I agree," Tony said.

"Well, that doesn't bode well for us," Battle said. "If he's been planning this for all that time, he must have a contingency plan for every eventuality."

"Guys," Toombs said again. "There's a title on the new video."

They all looked at the laptop screen. Above the new square, in white font, three words had appeared.

David is found.

"Right, we need two teams ready to move," Battle said. "And another ambulance. Summers, you're still with me. Doctor, I want you with Morgan and Flowers. Get to the boy. If he's alive, talk to him and find out where he's been."

"And if he isn't?" Tony asked.

"There'll be a SOCO team on standby. Leave the crime scene to them if the boy's dead but glean any information you can from it first. The psychology of the killer and all that."

"Understood." Tony looked distressed. Dani knew he'd been affected by seeing the Goddard family's final moments. If he found David dead as well, she wasn't sure how he was going to handle it.

"I'll brief everyone," Battle said, "Keep your eyes on that screen." He left the office and strode across the IT floor to the exit.

"Are you all right, Tony?" Dani asked. The psychologist looked pale.

"Yeah, I'm fine," he said.

"If David isn't…with us anymore…let Flowers and Morgan handle it."

"I can't. I have to see everything. There'll be something of our man's personality at the scene. No matter how much planning he's done, he can't hide who he is."

Dani nodded. Tony was right; he had to see the scene, no matter how grisly it might be. She'd worked with the psychologist long enough to know he could gain insights about people from the tiniest details.

"I'll stay on the radio and let you know what's happening in the feeds," Toombs said. He spun around in his seat and took a radio off a charging dock.

He gave it to Tony. "Here, take this."

Tony took it and said, "How does it work?"

"Just press that button to talk. I'll put it on a private channel, so our conversation doesn't get lost in all the chatter. I'll let you know what's happening on the David feed."

"Thanks."

"I'll do the same with your radio," Toombs said to Dani, opening a window on his computer and typing into it.

Dani looked at the timers on the website. *0:32.10*. Time was slipping away.

Battle came back when there were less than five

minutes left. "All units are on standby. Now we wait for him to call."

Three minutes later, with the timers showing less than two minutes left, there was still no call from dispatch.

"Why isn't he calling?" Battle said frustratedly.

"He's keeping us off balance," Tony said. "Just when we think we know what he's going to do, he switches it up."

The timers reached one minute.

"Come on," Battle muttered under his breath. "Tell us where they are."

0:48.03

The squares on the screen expanded and sat side by side. The feeds began but only showed static.

0:46.34

Dani gripped the back of Toombs' chair, her knuckles turning white from the pressure.

0:28.02

The seconds seemed longer than usual, as if time had elongated. Dani needed to see something on the feeds, needed to know what they were dealing with.

0:11.22

Dani felt her heart hammering in her chest.

0:08.01

She wanted to make a move, needed to be in motion. Someone was in danger, and she was standing here doing nothing. But without more information, there was nothing she could do. She felt helpless.

0:00:00

The static cleared and the images in both feeds became visible.

On the left, the feed showed the interior of a warehouse. In the centre of the space sat a large Perspex tank that looked at least eight feet tall. Lying on the bottom of the tank, tangled in fishing nets, was a dark-haired man. His eyes were wide with fear, and he struggled against the thick nets that weighed his body down.

The tank was sealed. Water trickled in from a pipe connected to one wall. The water level was no more than an inch deep at the moment, but it wouldn't be long before it covered the man tangled in the net.

The image on the other feed was of twelve-year-old David Goddard. The boy was thankfully alive and didn't appear to be in immediate danger. He was inside what looked like a wooden shack. David was sitting on a wooden dining chair in the middle of an empty room. Although he didn't seem to be restrained or tied to the chair he sat there quietly.

"Where the hell are they?" Battle said. "Why hasn't he told us?"

Dani's phone buzzed. She checked the screen and saw a number she didn't recognise. This was not the time to be taking a call from a telemarketer or insurance salesman. She answered, ready to give the person on the other end an earful.

But as soon as she lifted the phone to her ear, a male voice said, "Hello, Detective Summers."

"Hello? Who is this?"

"Who I am doesn't matter right now. What matters is the man in the tank and the boy in the cabin."

She felt a chill wrap around her spine like a thread of ice.

"Listen carefully," the man continued. "The water tank is in unit 15, York Business Park. The boy is in a cabin in the forest near Sutton. Take the York Road out of the city and you'll see a sign. Hurry up, Detective Summers, the clock is ticking."

The line went dead.

"Unit 15, York Business Park," she told the others. "David is in the forest near Sutton. North on York Road."

Everyone moved at once, grabbing their things and leaving the office.

"Why the hell did he call you?" Battle said as they headed for the exit.

"I have no idea," she said.

The chill she'd felt when the man had spoken to her remained as she and Battle crossed the car park to his Range Rover.

Why had he rung her? And why had he killed her old partner? It was all starting to feel personal.

She couldn't think about that now. They had lives to save.

CHAPTER
ELEVEN

They sped across the outskirts of the city to the York Business Park. Battle's Range Rover headed the convoy of police and emergency vehicles, followed closely by patrol cars, unmarked detective vehicles, a SOCO van, and an ambulance.

Dani was on her radio, speaking to Toombs.

"The water is still trickling slowly into the tank," the IT technician said. "You should get there in plenty of time."

"What about David?" She knew she should be focussing on the man in the tank but couldn't help asking about the boy.

"No change there. He's still sitting in the middle of the room. Shouldn't be too long until Tony and the others get there. Don't worry."

She knew Toombs meant well but she couldn't help worrying. So far, they hadn't managed to save anyone in the live feeds. The man who had set all of this up—the man who'd called her and given her the locations—was always a step ahead.

They reached the business park and found unit 15, a large warehouse surrounded by skips and piles of rubbish. The doors were two large steel sliding doors that were currently shut.

Battle and Dani got out of the Range Rover. He went to the doors. She spied a high window and scrambled onto a skip to reach it.

The glass was grimy, but she could see the tank in there. She couldn't see if the sliding doors were rigged in any way, though.

She jumped down and joined Battle. "I can't see if there are any wires, guv."

The DCI sighed. "Stand back. I'm going in."

She took a couple of steps back, as ordered, but no more than that. She was going in with him.

Battle grasped the door handle and tried to slide one of the doors. It slid easily, on metal runners. The DCI poked his head inside. "Looks clear."

He pulled on the door again and slid it open, revealing the interior of the warehouse.

The light spilling in through the doorway, as well as a couple of spotlights that had been mounted on the walls, illuminated the Perspex tank.

The man inside saw them through the Perspex and began to struggle harder against the heavy net that weighed him down.

The other vehicles were arriving now, skidding on the cement as they came to a stop outside the warehouse.

Battle and Dani were inside, rushing to the tank.

"How are we going to get inside, guv?" Dani said.

Battle was running back to the doorway. "We need cutting equipment! Where's that fire engine? We need the jaws of life," he shouted at the people outside.

He came back inside and marched over to something that stood by the doorway. Dani realised it was a camera on a tripod. This was where the live feed was coming from.

Battle picked up the tripod by the legs and swung the camera into the concrete floor. The device shattered. Battle threw the broken remains into the corner.

"No need for an audience," he said as he walked back to the tank.

Dani's radio crackled and Toombs' voice said, "The feed's gone dead."

"Don't worry about it," Dani told him. "We've disabled the camera. Concentrate on David."

She heard a rushing sound in the pipes above their head. "What's that?"

"Sounds like water," the DCI said.

The trickle of water that had been running down the inside wall of the tank suddenly became a torrent. It gushed over the man and the nets.

"We need that equipment now!" Battle shouted towards the doorway. His eyes scanned the pipework on the ceiling frantically. "How do we turn it off?"

Dani searched the pipework for a valve or a cut-off switch. Anything that would halt the flow of water.

It was rising over the struggling man's face now. His eyes were wide with terror. He shouted and screamed but the Perspex was so thick and the rushing of the water so loud that his voice was lost.

A uniformed officer ran in with an axe. He swung it at the tank. The axe blade embedded itself in the thick Perspex but didn't break through. The officer pried it loose and swung it again with the same result.

The man inside was underwater now, thrashing desperately against the nets.

Dani ran outside, desperate to find a tool that would get them into the tank. A fire engine was arriving, coming to a stop behind the ambulance. She ran over to it and shouted, "We need the jaws of life. Now!"

A fireman jumped down and grabbed the hydraulic cutters. He sprinted after Dani into the warehouse.

When she got inside, Dani's heart fell. Battle and the uniformed officer were standing by the tank with grim expressions on their faces.

The tank was full of water.

The man lying at the bottom, beneath the nets, was no longer struggling. His dead eyes stared out through the Perspex.

"It's too late," Battle said.

"No, it can't be." Dani couldn't accept that

they'd been beaten again. That another person had died.

"Cut through the tank," she told the fireman. "We need to get him out of there."

He nodded and walked over to the tank. He examined the smooth surface, considering where to place the first cut.

"Wait a minute," said a voice from behind them.

Dani turned to see Ian Radcliffe standing inside the doorway.

"There's a lever on the wall there," he said, pointing. "Looks like it's connected to the tank."

Dani followed his gaze to a lever on the wall. Insulated cables ran from the lever to the rear of the tank. She hadn't taken any notice of them before because her attention had been concentrated on the tank and the pipes.

Radcliffe stepped up to the lever and examined it. He followed the cables to the back of the tank and nodded. "There are small incendiary devices on the tank back here." He returned to the lever and said, "Stand back."

Everyone stepped away from the tank.

Radcliffe pulled the lever, and a series of small *pops* filled the air. Then the rear wall of the tank fell away and clattered to the cement. Water gushed out over the warehouse floor.

"Get the paramedics in here!" Battle shouted.

Two paramedics—a man and a woman—rushed in and entered the tank through the missing rear section. They bent down to examine the man in the fishing nets, checking for vital signs.

The woman looked up at Battle and shook her head slowly.

The DCI turned away and left the building, his head low.

Dani looked at Radcliffe. "How did you know that lever was there?"

"I saw it when I came in."

"Did you? I didn't. The guv'nor didn't."

"What are you saying?"

She wasn't sure exactly *what* she was saying. She just found it odd that Radcliffe noticed a lever straight away that she and the DCI had missed because they'd been focussed on the man in the tank.

Anyone entering the warehouse would have their attention drawn to the Perspex tank and its occupant, not anything else.

Unless they were specifically *looking* for something else.

Even as the thought entered her head, she wasn't sure what it signified. That Radcliffe knew the lever was there before he entered the warehouse? That wasn't possible, unless he'd already known about the warehouse and the tank.

"I'm not saying anything," she said. "Sorry. I'm just frustrated because if we'd known about the lever earlier, we could have saved that man's life."

She turned away—making a mental note to look into Ian Radcliffe and find out if he was connected to this case in more ways than he was letting on—and walked out of the warehouse.

The Counter Terrorism officer stood alone by the tank as the fireman and uniformed officer cut through the nets that weighed the dead man down.

When she got outside, she pushed through the crowd of detectives, uniforms, and firemen to find Battle sitting in his Range Rover.

She climbed into the passenger seat and closed the door.

"Are you all right, guv?"

"No, I'm not bloody all right. This bastard has got us running round like blue-arsed flies and all we've got to show for it is more dead people. He's ten moves ahead of us."

"He'll make a mistake eventually," she said, attempting to reassure him. "They usually do."

"Not this fellow. He's planned everything so meticulously. He even felt confident enough to put a lever that blew the tank open right there in plain sight because he knew we'd miss it."

"We can't blame ourselves for that, guv. We were focussed on trying to save someone's life."

"And the means to do so was on the wall next to us."

"We couldn't have known that."

He sighed and shook his head. "He's playing us for fools."

He picked up his radio and said, "Toombs, what's happening with the boy?"

"Nothing yet," Toombs said. "He's still sitting there. Tony's team are still on their way."

Battle put the radio on the dashboard and turned to face Dani. "They'd better save him. If anything good is to come out of this day, then they'd better save David Goddard."

―――――

Tony sat in the passenger seat of DS Lorna Morgan's Saab as it sped north out of the city towards Sutton. Matt Flowers sat in the backseat. The atmosphere in the car was tense and quiet. Everyone knew that a child's life depended on them.

"Anything to report, Chris?" Tony said into the radio. The silence in the car was putting him on edge.

"Nothing yet," Toombs replied. "He's still just sitting there."

At least he's alive, Tony thought.

"How do we know where the cabin is?" Lorna said.

"He said we'll see a sign."

"What? An actual road sign?"

"I have no idea."

Tony looked in the wing mirror and saw the three police cars following them. They didn't have their lights or sirens on, but they were sure to be noticed by someone. And then the media would be on their way, looking for a story.

He hoped this story would have a happy ending.

"I just got a text from one of my mates in the support team," Matt said from the backseat. "They couldn't save the bloke in the tank. The water started gushing in as soon as the DCI and Dani arrived. Battle went crazy. Smashed up the camera."

Tony and Lorna didn't reply. Tony knew they were both thinking the same thing: *We're not going to be able to save David, either. The game is rigged to make sure we lose.*

"Sign ahead," Lorna said.

Tony saw it at the same time she did. A wooden, square sign posted at the side of the road. Painted on it in black, capital letters were the words, *Boy in cabin. Next right.*

"We'll need to canvass motorists along this stretch of road," Matt said. "Someone might have seen him putting that up."

It was worth a try, but Tony doubted it would yield any results. "He's much too clever to be spotted while setting up the game."

"Is that what you think this is, Doc? A game?"

"To him it is. We're just playing pieces that he's moving around a board. He tells us where to go and we go."

"There are people in danger," Matt said. "We don't have a choice."

"No, we don't. He's manipulating us every step of the way."

"Next right coming up," Lorna said.

Up ahead, a right turn was marked with a white

arrow. Below the arrow, on an oblong piece of wood, were the words, *Tick Tock.*

Tony balled his hand into a fist and slowly released the pressure in an attempt to stay calm. They were being led into a trap, there was no doubt about that. The only question that remained was who would live and who would die today.

He balled his hand into another fist.

The road—which was nothing more than a wide track that was probably used by forestry vehicles—cut through the trees. Tall pines towered over the cars as the police convoy proceeded deeper into the forest.

"Isn't there supposed to be an ambulance with us?" Tony asked, checking the wing mirror again and seeing only police cars. He felt suddenly distressed that there was no ambulance close by.

"It's delayed," Matt said. "Someone back there is in contact with them, letting them know where we are."

"Right." Tony wasn't reassured by that at all. His fear that today was going to end in tragedy had heightened since they'd entered the forest. It gnawed at his stomach and made him feel sick.

The Saab rumbled over the uneven track. It was dark in the forest, beneath the canopy of foliage, and Tony felt suddenly cold. He knew that was more to do with the creeping fear he felt than the absence of sunlight in this place.

They drove along the track for fifteen minutes before it ended in a circular area of compacted dirt.

There was another sign here. This one depicted a large smiley face, painted black on a white background. Beneath the face were the words, *David is found*.

"Same as the title on the video feed," Lorna said. "But where's the cabin?"

Tony keyed the radio. "Chris, we're here. What's happening?"

"Nothing new," the technician's voice said. "Wait a minute. Another window is opening up. I can see you. There's a camera somewhere in front of you. I can see a Saab and three police cars."

"What about David?"

"Still the same."

"What do we do?" Matt said. "There's nothing here."

"Wait a minute," Toombs said. "I'm going to check a map of the area."

The radio went dead for a few seconds, then Toombs said, "There's a campsite north of your location. It closed down some time ago, but there are three cabins there."

"That's the place," Tony said. "How do we get there?"

"I can see a trail leading through the trees. Should be to your left."

Tony leaned forward in his seat and squinted at the trees to the left of the car. He couldn't see any trail.

Taking the radio, he got out and walked forward into the wide circular area, which had obviously once served as a car park for the now disused campsite.

A narrow dirt trail led into the forest.

"Found it," he told Toombs. "Stay in touch."

"I will, Tony. A third window has opened, and I can see you standing there. Must be a camera in one of the trees."

"So, he's going to broadcast everything live."

"Yeah, and there are a lot of viewers. More than ten thousand."

Tony returned to the cars, feeling a tinge of despair mixed in with the fear that now sat in his belly like a hard knot. He knew that most of those ten thousand people were watching because they wanted to see something terrible happen. It was morbid curiosity that had brought them to the website.

He signalled to the uniformed officers. They got out of their cars and assembled in front of him, along with Matt and Lorna.

"Someone needs to wait here for the ambulance," he said. "The rest of us are going along that trail. There's a disused campsite up there. That's where David is."

He wasn't sure why Battle hadn't put him in charge of this operation. He had no rank over these people—he had no rank at all—yet they all seemed willing to follow his orders. One of the uniforms—a young man named PC Flinn—offered to wait for the ambulance and the others gathered at the trailhead.

"By the way, we're being filmed," Tony told Matt

and Lorna as they walked over to the where the officers waited.

"Great," Matt said. "That's all we need."

"Everyone be careful," Tony said as he stepped onto the trail, followed by the two detectives and the uniformed officers. "We don't know what to expect."

They moved deeper into the forest.

CHAPTER
TWELVE

The trail took them on a winding path through the trees before ascending a shallow incline. A wooden sign sat at the base of the incline, but this was an old sign that had been here for years.

Sutton Forest Campsite. Tents and Cabins. No Fires.

"This is the place," Matt said.

They climbed the incline and found a large clearing at the top. A small brick building, which may have been the campsite shop at one time, sat to their left. The door was hanging on one hinge and Tony could see that the interior was full of old timber piled haphazardly on the floor.

A white sign stood in the centre of the clearing. Something was written on it, but it was too far away to be seen clearly.

At the far edge of the clearing, three cabins sat together beneath high, overhanging branches. A large white number had been painted over the door of each building.

1

2

3

There was nothing to indicate which cabin David was in.

As a group, they moved across the clearing to the sign.

Choose wisely.

"What's that supposed to mean?" said one of the uniforms. "Apart from the numbers, they're all the same."

Tony looked at the cabins. They were identical. Each had a wooden porch and a single wooden door. The windows were boarded up.

"What are we supposed to be figuring out?" Matt said.

Tony let out a slow breath. They'd been drawn into a game of chance. "There's nothing to figure out," he said. "There *is* no wise choice, despite what the sign says. It's entirely random."

"Are you sure?" The detective narrowed his eyes at the three identical cabins. "Everything he's done so far has been calculated. He hasn't brought us all the way here just to leave everything to chance."

"I agree. He hasn't." He pressed the button on the radio. "Chris, what's happening?"

"David is still sitting quietly, and I can see you standing by the sign."

Tony looked around for a stick. He found one that had some weight to it and threw it at the door of cabin 1. It clattered against the wood and fell to the porch.

"Did David hear that?" he said into the radio.

"If he did, he didn't react in any way."

Tony repeated the action, this time throwing a stick at the second cabin. "How about now?"

"Nothing," Toombs said.

Tony threw a stick at cabin 3. Toombs reported that there was still no reaction from the boy.

Matt came over to Tony. "What's the plan, Doc?"

Tony considered for a moment. "I don't think David is in any of the cabins."

"What? He must be. The sign says choose wisely."

"Yes, it does. But it doesn't say to choose one of the cabins, does it?"

Matt looked back at the sign and at the cabins. "Well, no, but I assumed..." His words trailed away.

"We all assumed," Tony said. "That's what he wants, for us to assume things. That's how people have been killed. David isn't here."

Matt waved his arms at the cabins and the sign. "What's all this, then?"

"A misdirection. Look at what happened to the Thompson family. The police were distracted by the fact that a family was in danger inside the house that they barged in and blew the place up. Then there's the Goddards. The police were thinking about what happened last time, so they waited. And the Goddard family died."

He shook his head. "These cabins and numbers are the distraction this time. If we go blundering into any of them, they'll probably blow up, or they'll be some other type of trap."

"Where the hell is David, then?"

Tony closed his eyes and replayed their journey since turning onto the forest track. There had been a sign that had said, *Tick Tock*, meaning time was of the essence. Then the smiley face at the car park and the words that matched the title of the video feed. *David is found*.

Tony keyed the radio. "Chris, what is David doing?"

"No change, Doc. He's just sitting there."

David hadn't been poisoned; if he had, he'd probably be dead by now like the rest of his family, or he'd be showing signs of some sort of illness.

So why *Tick Tock*? If David wasn't poisoned, why was time of the essence?

And why was David sitting still in the chair? Why wasn't he trying to find a way out of the room? Had the man who'd put him there instilled so much fear in the boy that he didn't dare move?

Possibly, but that didn't explain the sign.

Tick Tock

Time running out.

Tick Tock

David sitting quietly in the chair. Trying not to move.

Tick Tock

Trying not to breathe.

Sudden realisation came to Tony. He felt a shot of adrenaline course through his blood. "We're wasting time here!" he shouted. "Everyone follow me!"

He sprinted back to the path that had led them here.

Matt followed closely. "Doc, what is it? Where are you going?"

"David isn't moving because he's trying to preserve his air. He's underground."

"No, he can't be. Dani was told he'd be in a cabin."

"A cabin isn't only a house in the woods. It's also a room on a boat. A room beneath the deck."

Matt went quiet for a moment as they ran along the trail. Then he said, "But where?"

"Where we saw the sign."

They reached the car park and Tony pointed at the sign with the smiley face.

David is found.

"He's under there," Tony said, pointing at the ground beneath the sign. Now that he was looking closely at it, he could see the soil had been disturbed.

"We need to dig here," he shouted at the officers as they emerged from the forest.

Tony noticed something in the undergrowth. He stepped towards it and picked it up. A garden spade. It didn't look new, but Tony was sure it had been placed here recently.

No time to bag it as evidence; if they were going

to get to David before his air ran out, the spade had to be put to use.

He thrust the blade into the loose earth and started to dig.

The uniformed officers dropped to their knees and began to dig with their hands, moving the loose earth quickly.

Toombs' voice came from the radio. "Tony, you're in the right place. David is looking up towards the ceiling. He can hear you."

That spurred Tony on. He plunged the spade into the ground again and again and threw the soil over his shoulder. When he was knee deep in the hole, he leaned on the spade handle and gasped for breath.

Matt took the spade from him. "I'll take it from here, Doc."

Tony clambered out of the hole and leaned against a tree to support himself while he caught his breath. He made a silent promise to himself that he'd join a gym or take up running. He needed to do something—*anything*—to improve his fitness.

"Find!" an officer shouted.

Tony returned to the edge of the hole to see the man sweep soil away from wood.

Matt took over with the spade, revealing more wood beneath the earth. After a couple of minutes of digging, he uncovered an eight-foot by eight-foot square of thick timber. A trap door sat in the centre, with a dull metal ring that served as a handle to pull it open.

CHAPTER TWELVE 111

"Everyone get back," Matt said.

The officers climbed out of the hole and stood a few feet away.

"Chris, what's happening," Tony said into the radio.

"He's standing up and looking up at the ceiling."

Matt pulled the trap door open.

There was no explosion, no poison gas, no arrows shot from holes in the trees. Just David Goddard looking up at them from within a wooden box that had been sunk into the earth.

Matt reached down to him, and the boy took his hand. The detective pulled David out of his wooden prison and said, "You're safe now."

He guided David towards Tony and lowered himself into the sunken box to check it for clues.

Tony reached for David and helped him out of the hole. "Come on, let's get you checked over." He guided the boy towards the ambulance, which had finally arrived and was sitting behind the line of police cars.

The paramedics saw Tony and David approaching and jumped out of the vehicle, opening the back door. One of them grabbed a blanket and brought it over to the boy, swaddling him in it.

"These people will take good care of you," Tony said.

"Are you one of the detectives?" David asked him.

"I'm a psychologist."

"Oh." The boy seemed disappointed. "I've got something I'm supposed to give to a detective."

"You've got something?"

David nodded.

"Well, you see that lady over there?" Tony pointed at Lorna, who was standing by the side of the hole. "She's a detective. Why don't you give me whatever it is you've got and I'll make sure she gets it?"

"No, I'm only supposed to give it to a detective."

"All right. Well then, I'll go and get her. Let these nice people check you over and we'll come over to the ambulance. How about that?"

David nodded again. "Okay."

The paramedic led the boy to the ambulance while Tony went to get Lorna.

"Lorna," he said as he approached her. "David has got something that he'll only give to a detective."

"Let's have a look, then," she said, following him to the ambulance.

When they got there, David was sitting with his legs dangling over the rear bumper. He was still wrapped in the blanket, and the paramedic was shining a light into his eyes.

"Here's the detective I told you about," Tony said.

"Hi, David," Lorna said, smiling. "What have you got for me."

David reached into his pocket and held something out to her. "I'm supposed to give you this."

Lorna took it and held it in her fingers.
It was a small, black, plastic flash drive.

CHAPTER
THIRTEEN

Dani was sitting in the passenger seat of Battle's Range Rover, on the way back to headquarters, when Toombs' voice came over the radio.

"The boy is safe."

She felt a wave of relief wash over her. If nothing else, they'd managed to save David Goddard.

Battle picked up the radio. "Tell Dr Sheridan to question the boy. Find out what he knows."

"Don't you think we should give David time to recover?" Dani said to the DCI. "He's been through an ordeal."

"We need to question him while the details are still fresh in his mind. You know this, Summers, I shouldn't have to remind you."

She knew that eyewitness accounts were sharper in a victim's mind directly following an event, and that they faded with time, but she'd been thinking that David's mental welfare might be more important than any statement he could give.

CHAPTER THIRTEEN

The man they were chasing was meticulous to the last detail; Battle had said so himself. There was no way he'd reveal his identity to David, especially if he knew the boy would be talking to the police later.

The radio crackled. It was Toombs again. "We've got another flash drive. David Goddard gave it to DS Morgan."

"We'll be there in five minutes," Battle said, putting his foot down. The Range Rover accelerated, and Dani gripped the edges of her seat. She wondered if Battle, who had obviously not slept in the last 24 hours—should be driving at all, never mind racing along the outskirts of York.

She let out a breath of relief when they arrived at HQ and jumped out of the vehicle. She and Battle went up to the IT floor and found Toombs in his office, as well as Tony, Lorna, and Matt.

"Doctor, I want you to talk to David Goddard," Battle said. "Find out what he remembers."

"I can't, boss," Tony said. "He's been sedated."

Battle looked like he was about to argue, then his face softened. "Well, as soon as he wakes up, then."

He turned to Toombs. "What's this about another flash drive?"

The technician held up the small, plastic device. "David had this in his pocket. He'd been told to give it to a detective."

"All right, let's have a look."

As Toombs pushed the flash drive into the

laptop, Dani felt her muscles tense. She half expected some grisly scene to appear on the screen.

A video file appeared, which did nothing to allay her fear that she was about to watch something gruesome, but when Toombs clicked the file, the video showed nothing more than a white screen.

Then a voice began to speak. It was a man's voice, digitally altered to remove any identifying characteristics.

"This is the GameMaster speaking. You call yourselves guardians, bringers of justice, protectors of the innocent, but you are none of these things.

Your actions cause more harm than good, as you have now shown to the world with your failed rescue attempts of the Thompson and Goddard families."

An image appeared onscreen. A photo of the inside of the Thompson house, showing the wired front door and the living room.

"If any of the officers arriving at this scene had looked through this window, they would have seen the wires and realised that the only safe way to enter the house was through the back door, or through any of the windows."

A red arrow appeared, pointing at the living room window. Then the image switched to a photo of the back door, which hadn't been booby-trapped.

"Fools rush in. And now the Thompson family is gone."

The image disappeared, to be replaced by a photo of a bedside table with four loaded syringes sitting on it.

"Mrs Goddard's bedside table. If you had reached the family in time, the antidotes to what was in their system

was sitting right there next to the bed. Injecting them with it would have given you more than enough time to get them to the hospital."

A red arrow pointed at the syringes.

"Your ineptitude caused you to wait too long outside the house. Fools hesitate, detectives."

"There's no way we'd inject someone with an unknown substance," Battle grumbled. "He knows that."

"Since you are watching this video, you found David Goddard alive and well. You are probably congratulating yourselves on a job well done. It's nothing more than a game to you."

The screen turned black.

"Just remember that now, you're playing my *game. And I make the rules."*

The video ended.

"Right," Battle said. "What do we make of all that?" He looked from face to face, then his gaze settled on Tony. "Doctor?"

Tony narrowed his eyes, thinking. "There's a lot to unpick out of that diatribe, but one thing that stands out to me is his assumption that we found David alive. He recorded this before he put the boy in the box, and we'd still have this video even if we'd found David's dead body because it was in his pocket. So how did he know David wouldn't run out of air?"

"The box was ventilated," Matt said. "There was a grille on the wall behind David, near the floor. A pipe ran underground from there and was poking up through the surface a few feet away, in the woods. There was plenty of air."

"And you're only telling us this now?" Tony said.

"You were talking to the paramedics at the time. I didn't think it was that important."

"It's of vital importance," the psychologist said. "It's a piece of the puzzle."

Matt shrugged. "I don't see it, myself."

"This guy will kill anyone without a second thought," Tony said, waving his hand at the now-blank laptop screen. "Women, children, he doesn't care. But he has this boy for over 24 hours, and he doesn't harm a hair on his head. Why not?"

"I don't know," Matt said.

"No, you don't. And neither do I. But the fact is, he broke his pattern for David. The Thompsons, the Goddards, the man in the water tank. All dead. He made sure of that. He might pay lip service to giving us a way of saving them, but that's all bollocks, and he knows it. He made sure they died. But he made sure David *lived*. He's revealed a part of himself to us, perhaps unwittingly. It's important."

"All right, Doc, I'm sorry. I should have told you sooner," Matt said.

Tony turned to Toombs. "Can you get me a transcript of that video?"

The technician nodded. "Of course."

"Anybody else have anything to offer?" Battle asked.

"What about the fact that he's communicating

with us at all?" Dani said. "Surely that means something. Why is he doing it?"

"Attention, most likely," Matt said.

"It's not only that," Tony said. "Sure, he likes attention. That's why he's broadcasting all of this on the Net. But there's something more to it than that. Something personal."

"It felt personal when he rang me," Dani said. She was still creeped out by the fact that the GameMaster knew her personal number. He was a whiz with computers, so it shouldn't come as a surprise that he could find out anyone's number he wanted, but why hers?

"Yes, I've been thinking about that," Tony said. "The GameMaster might be someone you and Greg put away when you worked together."

"That's a lot of people," she said.

"If you think back to that time, does anyone stick out as being particularly aggressive or anti-police?"

She cast her mind back to when she and Greg worked together but it was a long time ago and nothing stuck out to her. "It was over a decade ago," she told Tony. "I can't think of anyone who would hold a grudge all these years and then do this."

"It's an angle worth investigating," Battle said. "We'll get someone in the support team to go through your old case files."

Dani nodded. She didn't envy anyone that task. Case files were hardly exciting reading material.

"I'd like to have another word with Helen Hughes," she said. "Get more details about what was going on around the time Greg went missing."

"Good idea," the DCI said. "Something might have been overlooked at the time that makes more sense now we know about the GameMaster." He paused and said, "That name doesn't go beyond these four walls, got that? We don't need the press sensationalising this any more than they have already."

Everyone nodded. Dani—who'd had to deal with the media sensationalising the Snow Killer while she was hunting him—reckoned there'd be a lurid name in the papers soon, anyway, even if it was just something made up by a journalist with an overactive imagination. The press loved giving killers fancy names that sold papers and attracted social media clicks.

"I want everyone here bright and early tomorrow," said Battle. "This so-called GameMaster might think we're playing his game and don't have a hope in hell of catching him, but he's forgetting one thing: good, solid police work. That's how we're going to beat him."

He dismissed them and began talking to Toombs about analysing the flash drive.

Dani and Tony left the office together.

"Want to speak to Helen Hughes with me tomorrow?" she asked him.

"Of course. She makes a nice cup of tea."

Dani smiled. The psychologist might trivialise things sometimes, but he had a way with people that she herself had never mastered. It wasn't that he knew the right questions to ask, but rather that he knew *how* to ask them to get people to open up. She wasn't sure if he even knew if he was doing it, or if it just came naturally to him.

During the drive home, she went over old cases in her head, the ones she'd worked on with Greg. There were no particular incidents that stuck out, no spectacular event that would have spawned someone like the GameMaster.

The dogs were excited to see her as always and circled her relentlessly as she entered the cottage and made her way to the kitchen.

She fed them and opened the fridge to select a ready meal for herself. It was a choice between lasagna or tikka masala.

She chose the curry and placed it into the microwave. Deciding to exercise at least some cooking skill, she put a nan bread under the grill.

The meal was nothing to write home about, but when she'd eaten it, she felt full and that was all that mattered.

Barney and Jack were sitting by the front door, their intention clear.

Dani grabbed the leads and led them across the road to the moors. As she released the dogs and they bounded off over the heather, her phone rang.

She checked the screen.

Charlotte

"Charlie," she said, holding the phone close to her ear because it was windy on the moors.

"Hi, Mum. Where are you? It sounds like you're in a wind tunnel.

"I'm walking the dogs."

"Aww, give them a hug from me."

"I will when I get close enough. At the moment, they're haring over the moors like mad things. How's uni?"

"Fine. Nothing exciting. I'm glad it's my final year, to be honest."

"I thought you liked it there."

"Yeah, it's okay, but I'm ready to get a job. I've been working part time at MedCraft Pharmaceuticals, and they said they'll take me on full time when I graduate."

"Is that the field you want to pursue? Pharmaceuticals?"

"It's a good area for a chemist to get into. And MedCraft have a lab in Cornwall, so I could even end up moving down there."

Even further away, Dani thought. Since her daughter had gone to Birmingham University two years ago, she'd gradually become used to her not being at home anymore. But the thought of Charlie moving to the other end of the country hit hard, for some reason.

"Very nice," she said.

"You don't sound too pleased about it."

"I am. Cornwall's lovely." She knew her daughter had her own life to lead. She was no longer a child who needed nurturing and protecting; she was a grown woman with a bright future ahead of her.

Where had the time gone? It seemed like only yesterday that she and Shaun had brought baby Charlotte home from the hospital.

"It might not happen," Charlie said. "Not for a while, anyway."

"I'm pleased for you. How's Elliot?" Dani asked, steering the direction of the conversation to Charlie's favourite subject.

"He's fine. We're going to his parents' house this weekend. It's their wedding anniversary and they're having a big party."

"That'll be nice. If you two ever want to come up here, you know you're welcome. I'd love to see you."

"We'll come and see you soon, Mum. I just thought you'd be busy. There's been some stuff on the news."

"Yes, I'm busy, but I'm never too busy for you, Charlie. You know that."

"I know." She didn't sound convinced.

"Well, the offer's there," Dani said.

"Thanks. I've got to go, Mum. I'm going out for a pizza with friends."

"Okay. Enjoy yourself. Love you."

"Love you. Bye."

Dani put the phone into her coat pocket and sighed. Her life hadn't meant to be this way. She was supposed to grow old with Shaun. It had been hard since his death, and Charlotte moving away had made things even harder. She felt like she'd lost her daughter as well as her husband.

Barney and Jack came running back to her, tails wagging and tongues lolling. They circled her once and then ran off again, inviting her to join in their game of chase.

While it might be a good way to burn off the tikka masala, Dani was in no mood to go running today. She felt tired. She planned to get back home, watch something on telly that required no brain power, and go to bed early.

There was a Regency Romance novel on her bedside table that she'd meant to start reading for the past couple of months. Now was as good a time as any.

"Come on, boys," she called to the dogs as she turned around and headed back towards the cottage.

They scampered past her, barking at each other as they wheeled and darted over the heather and grass.

As they got closer to home, Dani saw a car parked on the road outside her cottage. She didn't recognise it and from this distance, she couldn't make out any details regarding the make or model, or who was inside. She could barely see anything other than the headlights.

The vehicle sat there, outside her cottage, for a couple of minutes, and then—as Dani and the dogs got closer—drove away.

When she reached the road, she looked in the direction the car had gone. No sign of it now. Just the dark, empty road cutting through the moors.

CHAPTER
FOURTEEN

Tony picked up his and Alina's tea from a Chinese takeaway on the way home.

When he entered the establishment—where half a dozen people sat on white plastic chairs along the walls, waiting for their orders—he was greeted with a cheery, "Tony, good to see you," from Delun Li, a teenager who worked behind the counter and knew Tony well.

"Hi, Delun." Tony perused the menu on the counter for a couple of seconds, but he knew what he was going to order. It was what he always ordered: sweet and sour tofu balls for Alina and a chicken curry for himself, along with spring rolls and fried rice.

He told Delun what he wanted, and the teenager wrote it on a slip of paper, which he passed through to the kitchen, where his parents cooked the food.

"I saw you on the TV today," Delun said. "You're a hero, Tony!"

"What? No, I'm not. What do you mean?"

Delun pointed at an old TV set behind the counter that was currently tuned to the BBC. The six o' clock news was on, and a politician was in the studio, debating something with Sophie Raworth.

"You were on just a minute ago. You saved that boy. There was a video of you pulling him out of the ground."

"Oh, that. It wasn't just me. There was a team of us there."

"All I know is you are a hero, Tony, and you eat free tonight."

"Really, Delun, that's not necessary."

"I insist."

Tony found an empty seat and sat down, amid curious stares from the other customers. Ten minutes later, when Delun appeared from the kitchen and called Tony's name, some of the customers who'd been there before him changed their expressions from curiosity to animosity. It was obvious to everyone that Tony's order had been pushed to the front of the queue. Delun also tossed in a free bag of prawn crackers.

When he got back to his Mini, Tony turned the radio on and heard his name coming from the speakers.

"…saved by Tony Sheridan. The moment that he saved the boy was witnessed by thousands on the Internet. Dr Sheridan is the man who caught the Lake Erie Ripper in Canada and—"

Tony switch to a music station. He drove home listening to eighties pop hits.

When he opened the door of his flat, he found Alina sitting on the sofa in front of the telly. She was watching the news; specifically, the footage of Tony pulling David Goddard out of the sunken room.

"Tony, you are all over the news," she said. "You saved that boy. You must feel proud."

"It wasn't just me," he said, placing the takeaway bag on the kitchen table. "What you can't see on that video is Matt Flowers helping David from below."

"But you worked out where he was," she said, getting up and coming over to him. She kissed his cheek. "I am proud of you, even if you are so modest. You know about the cabins, right?"

"The cabins? What about them?"

"They were wired with explosives. If you had chosen any of them, people would have been killed. You not only saved the boy's life, but you also saved the lives of police personnel."

"I didn't know that."

"There was a press conference. The superintendent mentioned you many times."

He went to the cupboard and got some plates. Alina watched him closely as he set them on the table.

"You do not like being a celebrity, do you?"

"Not really. This has happened before. I didn't like it then, either."

"In Canada?"

He nodded.

"Tony, you help a lot of people. When that involves sending killers to jail, or saving innocent children, it is bound to draw attention to you."

"That doesn't mean it's welcome attention."

"I know. You would rather that it did not happen, but I'm afraid it is something you will have to live with. At least until it blows over and the media focusses on someone else."

He took the hot, foil trays out of the bags and placed them on the table. "The Chinese takeaway gave me this for free."

"Well, that is nice of them. It is a gesture of appreciation."

She got the cutlery out of the drawer and brought it over to the table. "You are a good man fighting against evil. That is a struggle that interests everyone. Would you rather be a dentist? Or a plumber?"

"No, I like helping people."

"Then you just have to view this unwanted attention as an occupational hazard. There is nothing you can do about it, and the positives of your job outweigh the negatives."

"You're right," he said. "I can live with it."

She smiled. "Good. Now, what do we have here?" She indicated the foil trays.

"Sweet and sour tofu balls."

"My favourite."

They ate and talked. Tony told her about his day

and Alina said she was going to pop into work tomorrow to see how everyone there had been getting on without her.

In the background, the news continued and at one point, Tony heard one of the presenters say, *"Solomon Gantz, better known as the Lake Erie Ripper, is in prison thanks to Tony Sheridan. Many women owe their lives to the forensic psychologist, including two young women he personally saved from the Ripper's house."*

He mentally tuned the presenter's voice out and concentrated on the woman sitting in front of him. Tomorrow was Alina's last day here before she returned to the Viking dig in Sussex. He was going to miss her.

"Do you know how much longer the dig will take?" he asked.

"No more than a few weeks," she said. "Maybe a month. It depends what else we find down there."

He nodded and went back to eating his curry.

"It won't be long, Tony. I can come and visit again in the meantime, or you could take a few days and come to Sussex. I've told everyone on the team about you and they're dying to meet you."

"I'd like that," he said. "When this case is over, of course."

"Yes, of course." She reached across the table and took his hand in hers. "Don't worry, it will be over at some point. You'll catch this man. I am sure of it."

He wished he could share her faith. So far, the

GameMaster was holding all the cards and Murder Force had an empty hand.

After they finished the takeaway, Alina put the kettle on, and they drank tea while watching a comedy with Ryan Reynolds and Dwayne Johnson. For a while, Tony forgot all about the GameMaster and the website that broadcast live videos of murders and enjoyed being with Alina and watching her laugh.

Later, when a nightmare woke him in the middle of the night, he heard her sleeping soundly next to him and relaxed into his pillow.

In the nightmare, he'd been walking along a dimly lit corridor to a steel door that had the word GameMaster spray painted on it in red.

Tony had opened the door to reveal a hooded figure sitting behind a desk. A chess board sat on the desk and there were only four pieces left on the board: a white knight, a white queen, a black bishop, and a black king. Even though he was dreaming, he knew the configuration on the board couldn't be right, because once one side loses its king, that side has lost.

The hooded figure raised its head to look at Tony. He couldn't see the face, only dark shadows.

The figure raised its hands and pushed back the hood, grinning at Tony.

That was the point at which Tony had woken up with a start.

The face grinning at him from over chessboard had been the face of Solomon Gantz.

CHAPTER
FIFTEEN

"How was your evening?" Dani asked Tony as they drove to Helen Hughes' house. Tony had been sitting quietly in the passenger seat for the entire journey, first gazing out of the window, and then reading his notebook.

He looked up. "Hmm? Oh, fine. Just fine. You?"

"Fine," she said. She didn't mention the car that had been sitting outside her cottage, or the uneasy feeling she'd had for the rest of the night, going to the window to check for the vehicle every few hours.

The car hadn't returned.

"We had Chinese," Tony said, closing the notebook.

"Nice. I had curry and nan."

"You must be a keen cook. Curry last night, lasagna the night before."

She laughed. "They were ready meals. I can cook, but I don't really…have the time." She was going to say she didn't really see the point but changed her mind mid-sentence when she thought that made her sound too woe-is-me.

"Ah," Tony said. "Nothing wrong with a microwave special."

"Anything interesting in there?" Dani asked. Usually, Tony was brimming with theories about the unknown person who was the subject of their investigation—or the *unsub* as Tony sometimes said, using the FBI term—but lately, he'd been uncharacteristically quiet.

"I have to say, I'm drawing a blank at the moment," he said. "There are too many variables. He's killed families, individuals, and kidnapped a child. His actions are all over the place. It's hard to see a pattern."

"Maybe he's just acting randomly."

The psychologist shook his head and tapped his finger on the notebook. "No, there's a pattern. I just can't see it yet. It would help if we knew who the man in the water tank was, and how he's connected to the two families."

"What if he was just picked up off the street by chance? He's walking along the pavement, minding his business, and the next thing he knows, he's bundled into a van, taken to a warehouse, and thrown into a tank."

"It wasn't opportunistic. Everything the Game-Master does is planned out. I'm sure there's a meaning behind every detail." He sighed and placed the notebook in the door pocket. "It'll all become clear eventually."

When they knocked on the door of the house in Flanders Road, Helen answered with a look of confusion on her face.

"Dani, you're back."

"Helen, we'd like to ask you a few more questions, if we may."

"Of course, of course." She stepped back from the door, allowing them into the house. "I'll put the kettle on. Make yourselves at home."

Five minutes later, Helen was serving the tea. Tony was in the armchair and Dani was next to Helen on the sofa.

"I don't know what else I can tell you," Helen said, placing the teapot onto the tray. "I've already told you everything I know."

"We'd just like you to think back," Tony said. "Is there anyone who had a grudge against Greg?"

"There are the criminals he caught over the years, I suppose, but other than that, no one. Everybody liked Greg."

"Around the time he disappeared, did he mention bumping into someone from the past? Perhaps someone he hadn't seen for a decade or so?"

Helen shook her head. "No, nothing like that. I told you what I think happened. Someone Greg had put away saw him on the street and decided to get revenge. It was probably someone who'd just got out of prison and had built up a lot of resentment all that time they were inside. It can happen."

"But you have no idea who that could be?" Dani asked. "Greg didn't mention seeing anyone like that? Someone he'd put away in the past?"

"No, he didn't."

She looked at Tony and Dani closely. "You seem very eager to get to the bottom of this all of a sudden. Is it connected to another case?"

"We believe it could be connected to a case we're currently working on," Dani said.

Helen frowned. "You mean those families that were killed?"

Dani nodded.

"What's the connection?"

"We know that the person who set up the website that broadcast those crimes is in possession of Greg's driving licence."

"What?" Helen's hand flew to her mouth and her eyes widened. "I don't understand. Why would they have that?"

Tony leaned forward in the chair and softened his voice. "Mrs Hughes, did Greg have his driving licence on his person when he left the house?"

"Yes, of course. He had his wallet. He was going to the chemist."

"But it wasn't recovered when they found Greg on the beach."

"No. They assumed his wallet had been lost at sea." Tears sprang into her eyes as realisation struck. "So, it's true. He was murdered."

CHAPTER FIFTEEN

Dani took the woman's hand in hers as a gesture of comfort. Even though Helen had suspected for the past two years that her husband had been killed, having that suspicion confirmed must have come as a shock.

"You're saying the person who murdered Greg is the same person who killed those families?" Helen whispered.

"And the man yesterday," Dani said.

"What man yesterday?"

"It was on the news." Dani wasn't sure what details had been released to the press, but she knew yesterday's tragedy had been reported on the news, along with an artist's rendering of the victim's face. The police didn't have an ID for the man in the tank, and were appealing to the public for help.

"I haven't seen the news," Helen said. "I was at my church group yesterday and I was too tired to watch anything when I got home. I haven't put the telly on today."

"Oh," Dani said. She wasn't sure how to explain the events of yesterday to Helen. The man in the tank had drowned, just like Greg. Helen might get the idea in her head that Greg had been drowned in a tank as well, and his body dumped at sea.

Perhaps that was exactly what had happened.

Deciding that Helen would find out sooner or later anyway, Dani said, "A man drowned."

Helen's eyes widened. "Like Greg?"

"No, not in the sea. He was in a plastic tank."

"Oh my goodness, that's awful! Who was he?"

"We don't know yet."

Helen looked down at her hands and Dani could see her mind working. She was wondering if Greg had met the same end as the unknown man.

"Helen, it doesn't mean that's how Greg—"

"Tell me the details," Helen said. "I want to know everything."

"I don't think—"

"I want the details, Dani. If this is how Greg was killed, then I want to know exactly what happened."

Dani paused, gathering her thoughts.

She was about to explain yesterday's events when Tony came to her rescue, leaning forward in his chair and touching Helen's arm lightly.

"The man was in a tank that filled with water," he said gently. "He was held down by a pile of fishing nets."

Helen's brows furrowed. "Fishing nets?"

"That's right," Dani said.

"And they were piled on top of him?"

"Yes," Dani said. "Helen, there's no reason to believe the same thing happened to—"

"Wait a minute," Helen said, holding up a hand to silence Dani. "I need to think for a minute."

Dani and Tony were silent while Helen closed her eyes. Dani wondered if the poor woman was imagining Greg in a tank, stuck beneath a pile of fishing nets as water poured in from above.

"Do you have a picture of this man?" Helen asked.

"We have an artist's sketch," Dani said. She

wasn't about to show this distraught woman the photos from the crime scene.

"May I see it, please?"

"Here," Tony said, showing his phone to Helen. "This is the man."

Helen studied the artist's rendering, pursed her lips, and nodded. "His name is Frank Moseley."

"You know him?" Dani asked.

"Not really, no. Greg saved his life a couple of years ago. Not long before he disappeared, actually. Frank was homeless and was sleeping on the beach. A group of youths thought it would be funny to throw a pile of fishing nets on top of him and film it on their phones.

"They left him there, unaware that the tide was coming in. Or perhaps they were aware, who knows these days? Frank was tangled in the nets and unable to free himself. Luckily for him, Greg was walking along the beach early that morning—he'd had trouble sleeping the night before and had gone for a walk to clear his head. He saved Frank from drowning."

She got up and went to a bureau. Opening the drawers, she found what she was looking for and returned to the sofa with a newspaper clipping, which she gave to Dani.

Dani looked at the headline.

Retired Detective Saves Homeless Man's Life.

The article was accompanied by a black and white photograph of Greg at the side of a hospital bed.

The caption beneath the photo read, *Greg Hughes at the bedside of Frank Moseley, the man he saved from certain death.*

The photo was slightly faded, but there was no doubt that the man in the bed was the same man who had drowned in the tank yesterday.

"Do you mind if we keep this?" she said to Helen.

"If it will help with the investigation, you're welcome to have it."

Dani put the newspaper clipping into her bag. "You said Greg saved this man shortly before he disappeared?"

Helen nodded. "A week before, I think. I got the paper to send me the original of that photo. It's the last photo of Greg before he died."

"Did you ever meet Frank Moseley?" Tony asked.

"No. He was discharged from the hospital the next day and went back to living on the streets, as far as I know."

Until the GameMaster found him two years later, Dani thought.

"Did Greg mention anyone taking a particular interest in him rescuing Frank?" Tony asked.

She shook her head. "It was in the paper and mentioned on the local news, but it wasn't a big deal. Greg was never one for publicity."

That was true. Dani remembered Greg trying to avoid media attention whenever possible.

"Thank you, Helen," she said, getting up. "We'll stay in touch."

"All right," Helen said, seeing them to the door. "And remember, Dani, Greg was very proud of you. It was one of the last things he told me before he disappeared. He had faith in you and knew you'd catch the Snow Killer. Just like I have faith in you now and know you'll catch Greg's killer."

Dani gave her a thin-lipped smile. She wasn't going to make any promises.

When she got back in the Land Rover, she used the radio to call in the identity of the man who had died yesterday.

"Any thoughts?" she said to Tony as she started the Land Rover.

"I have lots of thoughts. Just let me get this down." He was writing in the notebook, which he'd left in the door pocket.

Dani turned around at the end of the road. She waved at Helen as they passed the house, wondering how the news about the tank was going to hit the poor woman once it settled into her mind.

They might *never* know exactly how Greg died, and in some ways, that made it worse for his loved ones. They could only speculate on the details and sometimes, the imagination was worse than reality.

Dani hoped that was the case, and that her old partner's death hadn't been too horrific.

Tony looked up from his notebook. "Have any members of the Thompson or Goddard families had any dealings with the police in the past?"

"You mean a criminal record? I don't think so."

"No, not as criminals. As victims of a crime."

"I have no idea. Do you have a theory?"

"Maybe." He picked up his radio and keyed it. "Chris, are you there?"

It only took a couple of seconds before Toombs replied. "I'm here, Tony. What's up?"

"Can you check the database and see if anyone from the Thompson or Goddard families has been involved in a crime in the past? Probably as a victim."

"Yeah, sure, I'll have a look."

"Thanks." Tony put the radio on his lap.

"You think they were victims like Frank Moseley?" Dani said.

"I can't find any other connection. If they've all been victims of a crime, it's something that ties them together."

Toombs came back ten minutes later, as they were driving out of the outskirts of Scarborough.

"Yeah, they've been involved with crimes," the technician said. "But they weren't victims, exactly."

"What do you mean?" Tony said.

"They were *potential* victims, but they weren't hurt in any way."

"Give me the details." Tony had the notebook open in his lap and his pen poised over it.

"Twelve years ago, Luke and Wendy Thompson lived in a house in York that had been divided into two flats. They lived in the first floor flat. An anonymous tip was phoned in to the police that the bloke who lived on the ground floor was storing explosives in his flat for a terrorist group."

Memories came flooding back to Dani. "I can tell you what happened next," she said. "Greg and I were in the area and our priority was to get the couple on the first floor clear of the building. We went upstairs and knocked on their door but while we were up there, the man on the ground floor saw our car parked in the street and realised he'd been rumbled. He set off the explosives."

"Really?" Tony said, his eyes wide with surprise. "What happened?"

"Before the explosion, Greg heard noises downstairs and realised what was about to happen. All four of us went out the kitchen window and jumped down onto a shed roof. If we'd gone back down the stairs, we'd have been done for. The explosion ripped the staircase apart and the entire first floor caved in."

"That's right," Toombs said.

"I didn't make the connection," Dani said. "That was Luke and Wendy Thompson."

Tony was scribbling in his notebook. "What about the Goddards, Chris?"

"Richard and Elaine Goddard were at a restaurant called the Blue Turtle ten years ago—"

"When the chef tried to poison everyone," Dani continued. "Greg and I got there before the ambulance. Everyone in the restaurant was dead or dying. We rushed four people to the hospital in our patrol car. Two of them didn't make it. Two of them had their stomachs pumped and survived."

She searched her memory for the names of the survivors.

"Spoiler alert," Toombs said. "The two people who survived were Richard and Elaine Goddard."

"So, all of this is connected," Dani said, feeling a chill creep up her spine. "The victims are people whose lives we saved."

"Got it in one," Toombs said.

"What happened to the chef at the Blue Turtle?" Tony asked.

"He poisoned himself as well as the customers," Dani said. "He didn't survive."

"And the guy who blew the house up?"

"They dug his remains out of the rubble. What was left of them, anyway."

"Damn it," Tony said, putting his pen down. "No suspects, just survivors."

"At least we have some idea about what's going on now," Toombs said from the radio.

"Yes," Tony said, looking down at his scribbled notes. "It's certainly intriguing."

Intriguing wasn't the word Dani would have used. The fact that someone was revisiting her old cases and changing the outcomes was terrifying.

CHAPTER
SIXTEEN

When they reached the outskirts of York, Tony's phone rang. He checked the screen and saw it was Battle calling.

"Hi, boss."

"Doctor, I want you and Summers to question the boy. He can't still be sedated. Get over to the hospital and find out what he knows."

"All right," Tony said, feeling a knot tighten in his stomach.

Battle hung up.

"What's up?" Dani asked.

"Battle wants me to talk to David Goddard."

She nodded. "Probably a good idea."

He sighed. "I doubt we'll learn anything useful. The GameMaster is too clever to reveal his identity to anyone."

"We'll know whether he is or not when we talk to David."

Tony said nothing. He folded his arms and tried

to breathe deeply to calm himself. After spending time in a mental institution in Canada, he couldn't set foot in a hospital without experiencing a sense of dread which turned into blind panic.

When Dani pulled into the hospital car park and killed the Land Rover's engine, Tony said, "Perhaps you should talk to him. I'll wait here."

She looked him over. "Are you all right?"

He felt clammy and shaky. He didn't feel all right at all. "I'm fine," he said.

"You don't look fine. What's the matter?"

He let out a long breath. "It's hospitals. I have a problem with them."

"With hospitals? I don't understand."

"After the Ripper thing, I was in a Canadian hospital for a while. A number of them, actually. It wasn't a good time. I'd been affected by what happened in his house. Solomon Gantz's house. Mentally, I mean. During my stay in one particular facility, I was hallucinating. Like I said, it was a bad time."

He realised he was rambling. His memories of the psychiatric hospital were vague, probably because of the cocktail of drugs he'd been on at the time, but even those drug-addled memories had planted a seed in his mind that had grown into a fully-fledged phobia.

He remembered a headline in the *Toronto Star*—*British Psychologist Loses Mind After Encountering Ripper*—and wondered if his subconscious feared he would lose his mind again if he set foot inside any place that was similar to those mental health facilities in Canada.

"Does Battle know about this?" Dani said.

He shook his head. "The only other person who knows is Tom Ryan. He helped me through a panic attack outside Whitby Hospital when we were working on the Abigail Newton case. He talked to me, distracted me."

"Do you want me to do that?"

"I don't think it would work. I'd know what you were doing. Ryan came out of nowhere and before I knew what was happening, I was in Abigail's room."

"If it's really that bad, Tony, I can go in there and you can wait here," Dani offered.

"Would you mind?" He felt weak, pathetic.

"I don't mind at all. Is there anything you want me to specifically ask David?"

"Not really. I know you'll ask the right questions."

She opened her door and got out. "See you soon." She closed the door and walked across the car park to the hospital building.

Tony felt his muscles relax. His breathing became more even and the trembling subsided. He felt bad about not accompanying Dani into the hospital but he also felt relieved that he didn't have to go in there.

He read through his notes again, particularly the ones he'd made after leaving Helen Hughes' house. The GameMaster was reversing the outcomes of cases Dani and Greg Hughes had worked on in the past, making sure the victims suffered the fate they would have all those years ago had Dani and Greg not intervened.

Tony couldn't see a motive. And why was the GameMaster doing all this now, all these years after the original events that had almost killed these people?

It didn't make any sense.

He mentally corrected himself. There was some kind of sense here somewhere, he just couldn't see it yet. Whatever motive was driving these crimes made perfect sense to the GameMaster.

"Why are you killing the people Dani and Greg saved?" he murmured. "What do you get out of it?"

He recalled the name of the website. *Will the police save them?*

"You're trying to show the viewers of those feeds that the police can't save everyone," Tony said. "But people know that. No one thinks the police are infallible."

No matter how much he needed to understand the motive behind the events that had taken place in the last couple of days, he couldn't. The GameMaster was an enigma.

"I'm back at square one," Tony said to himself.

He looked through the windscreen and was surprised to see Dani coming back across the car park.

She opened the driver's door and got in.

"That was quick," he said. "Is David still sedated?"

"He isn't there," she said, starting the engine. "His aunt took him home an hour ago."

"Do we know her address?"

Dani nodded. "She lives in Heslington. Shouldn't take us long to get there."

They drove south-east across the city, towards the University and York Science Park. Tony had been to Heslington once before, with Alina, and had found the suburban village charming, if busy. Due to its nearness to York University, the streets had been packed with students.

David Goddard's aunt lived on a street that was well away from the main road, however, and when Dani and Tony arrived, the place was quiet. The street consisted of mostly detached houses separated from the pavement by small, well-manicured lawns and neat, tarmac drives.

"Her name's Louise Slater," Dani said as they got out of the Land Rover. "Husband Alan. She's Elaine Goddard's sister. That's all I know."

Tony nodded. He had his notebook in hand this time. If David *did* have any information on the GameMaster, he wanted to make sure he wrote it down word-for-word.

Dani knocked on the door and a tall man in his fifties, wearing a dark blue jumper and jeans, answered.

"Alan Slater?" Dani said.

The man nodded.

Dani showed him her warrant card. "I'm DI

Danica Summers and this is my colleague, Dr Tony Sheridan. May we speak with David?"

"Yes, I suppose so. We were expecting someone from the police to come to the hospital but no one did."

"I'm sorry, sir, we've been very busy. And I was under the impression David was sedated for a while."

"Yes, he was. All right, come in." He stepped aside to allow them into the house, then led them to a large kitchen where David Goddard sat at a pine table while a woman with dyed blonde hair set a sandwich and a glass of orange juice in front of him.

She looked up when she saw Dani and Tony, then at her husband. "Police?"

Alan Slater nodded.

"It's about time. We thought you'd forgotten about poor David."

"Of course we haven't," Tony said. "We were told he was sedated."

"Yes, he was. Wouldn't you be sedated if you'd been kidnapped and then rescued, only to discover your entire family has been killed?" She lowered her voice when she said the last part, but Tony had no doubt David could hear her.

"Wait a minute," Mrs Slater said. "You're the man who rescued him. I saw you on the news. You're the psychologist who put that serial killer away in America."

"Canada," Tony said. "And it wasn't just me who rescued David. There was an entire team—"

"Come and sit down." She led Tony to the chair opposite David. "Would you like a cup of tea? How about a sandwich?"

"A cup of tea would be nice. We're both parched." He said the second part to remind Mrs Slater that Dani was also in the room.

"I'll put the kettle on." Mrs Slater went to sink and filled the kettle.

Tony looked across the table at David. The boy's eyes were red and dark circles sat under them. He looked older than his twelve years, and Tony knew that his recent experience would scar him for the rest of his life.

"Hi, David."

"Hello."

"Do you remember me?"

The boy nodded.

"I suppose you don't really want to remember what happened, do you?"

"I try not to think about it, but sometimes I can't help it."

"Of course. That's normal when something bad happens to us. It sticks around in our head for a while."

David nodded and looked down at the surface of the table.

"Do you think you could remember some things for me? Some really important things?"

"Okay."

"What's the last *normal* thing you remember? Before everything went wrong?"

"I remember going to bed. But when I woke up, I wasn't in my room."

"Oh? Where were you?" Tony wanted to open his notebook and write, but decided not to. He wanted this conversation to be as relaxed as possible. If he had to keep looking down at his notebook, he'd break the connection between himself and David.

"I didn't know at first. It was dark and everything was moving. Then I could see better in the dark. It was a van. The back of a van."

"Oh, right. Was there anything in that van? Apart from you, I mean. Was there anything else there with you?"

David nodded slowly, his gaze still fixed to the table. "There was a ladder. It was rattling around a bit. And there was a toolbox, like the one my dad has."

"I see. What about smells? What did it smell like in the back of the van?"

"It smelled funny. Like a sweet smell."

"Right. Like some kind of chemical?"

David nodded again.

Judging by the red marks on the skin under the boy's nose and around his mouth, Tony surmised the GameMaster had chloroformed the boy while he was asleep before bundling him into the van.

"I wanted to get away but my hands were tied behind my back and my ankles were tied as well."

"What happened next?" Tony said.

"The van stopped and the doors opened. There was a man standing there."

"Was he wearing a mask?"

David shook his head.

"Could you see his face?"

David nodded.

Tony felt a jolt of surprise. Had the GameMaster slipped up? He must have known that letting David see his face was a huge risk.

"Can you describe him, David?"

Tony looked over at Dani, glad to see that she had her notebook in her hand with her pen poised above it.

The boy nodded.

"Can you remember what colour his hair was?"

"It was blonde. Like mine."

"And what about his eyes? What colour were they?"

"Blue."

"Same as yours."

David nodded.

"Is there anything else about his face that you remember? Anything that sticks out in your memory?"

"He had a scar like Harry Potter."

"Oh? What did that look like?"

"Like a line on his forehead. Over his eyebrow."

"Right. Do you remember which side of his face it was on?"

The boy shook his head.

"What about his nose? Was it big or small?"

"Just normal size."

"His mouth?"

David shrugged. "Normal."

"Was he tall or short?"

Expecting the reply to be, "normal." Tony was surprised when David said, "He was tall."

"That's helpful. You're doing really well, David. Was the man as tall as your uncle?"

David looked over at his uncle. "He's taller than Uncle Alan."

"Oh, right. Was he thin?"

David shook his head.

"Fat?"

"No, he wasn't thin or fat. He was hench."

"Hench?" Tony wasn't familiar with the term.

"He means muscular," Mrs Slater said. "All the kids are saying it these days."

"Ah, I see. So, he was hench," Tony said to David. "Was he wearing something that showed off his muscles?"

"He was wearing a black jumper and black jeans."

"And what did he say to you, David? Did he speak at all?"

"He untied me and told me there was no point trying to run away because we were in the middle of a forest and there was nowhere I could run to."

"I see. What was his voice like?"

"A bit deep."

"Did he have an accent?"

David thought for a moment, then shook his head. "Not really."

"So, he sounded like he was from around here?"

The boy nodded.

"What did you see, David? What were the surroundings like?"

"Lots of trees."

"Nothing else?"

"A caravan."

"Can you describe it?"

"It was white and it had windows but they were black."

"Were they tinted?"

"No, they'd been painted with black paint."

Tony nodded his understanding. "And what happened next?"

"He made me beans on toast."

"In the caravan?"

"Yes."

"What was it like inside?"

David shrugged. "Like a caravan."

"Was it neat, or was it untidy?"

"Neat."

"Were there any pictures on the walls? Or personal items that belonged to the man?"

"No. I don't think he lives there. I think he just goes there sometimes."

"Why do you say that?"

"There wasn't much in there. Just some food in the cupboard and in the fridge, but not much."

"Did you eat the beans on toast?"

David nodded. "I was hungry."

"What did the man do while you were eating?"

"He kept saying stuff. Weird stuff that I didn't understand."

"Do you remember what he said?"

"He said I was special and I was going to have a hard life but I'd be better for it because I'd have to fight to survive and that would make me stronger." He shrugged. "I didn't get it."

Tony looked over at Dani to make sure she was taking all of this down. She was scribbling furiously in her notebook.

"What happened after you ate the beans on toast?"

"He said he had to go somewhere, so he chained me to a metal ring in the floor so I couldn't escape."

Mrs Slater's hand flew to her mouth and tears rolled down her cheeks. Her husband comforted her.

"It was a long chain," David said, seeing his aunt's distress. "I could move around the caravan and go the toilet when I needed to."

"Were you chained by the wrist?" Tony asked.

"My ankle. But he put padding around my ankle first, so it didn't hurt."

"And then he left the caravan?"

David nodded.

"Do you know what time it was?"

"No."

"Was it light or dark outside?"

"I don't know because the windows were painted black. I couldn't see outside."

"Did anything else happen while you were in the caravan alone?"

"No. I think I fell asleep. When I woke up, the man was back."

"Okay. Did he say or do anything?"

"He told me to go to bed because it was night time."

"Did he unchain you?"

"No. I went to bed but I didn't sleep for a long time. I kept thinking about my mum and dad and if they were looking for me."

Tony swallowed. The poor boy hadn't known at the time that his parents were dead.

"Where was the man while you were in the bedroom?"

"I don't know. I didn't see him again until the morning."

"So, he didn't…" Tony paused, wondering how to phrase the question, "…touch you in any way?"

"No. He touched my ankle to put the chain on, but that was the only time he touched me at all."

Mrs Slater let out a breath of relief and Tony realised that question must have been on her mind all this time.

"All right. So, what happened the next morning, when you saw the man again?"

"He gave me breakfast."

"What did you have?"

"Weetabix."

"Did he have breakfast as well?"

"No, just me."

"Did he say anything to you?"

"He said he was going to take me to a room later and that it was underground. He said I'd be okay as long as I sat on the chair and didn't move. He'd be watching me through a camera so he'd know if I moved."

"He said you'd be okay?"

"Yeah, he said the police would find me."

"And he gave you the flash drive."

"That was later, when he put me in the room. He told me to give it to a detective when I was found."

"I see. And you have no idea who this man was? You've never seen him before?"

"No, never."

"He didn't say anything that gave away his identity?" Tony knew the GameMaster was far too clever for that, but he had to ask anyway.

"No."

Tony looked over at Dani. "Do you have any questions?"

She shook her head. "I think we've got enough for now."

Tony looked back at the boy across the table. "Thank you, David. You did brilliantly."

David shrugged and gazed down at the table again.

Tony got up. "Right, we'll be on our way. Thanks for speaking to us, David."

"There was one other thing," the boy said, looking up.

Tony paused. "Oh? What's that?"

"Before he closed the trap door in the ceiling of the underground room, the man said he was sorry about everything, but it was all the police's fault."

"Do you remember exactly what he said, David?"

The boy closed his eyes, remembering. "I'm sorry things turned out this way, David, but it's all the police's fault. They've done this to you." David opened his eyes. "Then, he closed the door and I could hear soil hitting the ceiling."

Tony looked over at Dani. She was writing in her notebook.

"Thanks, David. If you remember anything else, or just want to talk, I'm going to give your aunt and uncle my phone number, okay?"

"Okay."

Tony gave his card to Alan Slater as the man saw them out.

"Take good care of him," Tony said, as he and Dani stepped outside.

"We will." Alan Slater thanked them and closed the door.

"What do you think that last part meant?" Dani said as they got into the Land Rover. "About the police doing it to David? Sounds delusional."

"He's projecting," Tony said. "That's why he let David live. He sees something of himself in the boy. Something happened to the GameMaster at some point in his life, and he blames the police."

"Lots of people blame us for things that are their own fault. They don't want to take responsibility, so they blame us."

"No, it's more than that. I think the Game-Master has survived some sort of tragedy. And he blames the tragedy on you and Greg."

CHAPTER
SEVENTEEN

"Blames it on us?" Dani said. "Why would he blame a tragedy on me and Greg?" She respected Tony's opinion, but to think that the events of the last few days had happened because the GameMaster blamed her and Greg for something sounded outlandish. They'd only ever tried to help people; they certainly weren't responsible for any tragedy.

"I don't know," Tony said. "But it's the only reason he'd tell David that everything was the police's fault."

"But why me and Greg?"

"Because everything that has happened so far is connected to you two. The families you saved together; the man Greg saved on the beach. The GameMaster has one aim: to destroy the good work you and Greg have done."

Dani cast her mind back to her time with Greg, trying to remember a tragedy that had happened on their watch. "In police work," she told Tony, "lots of bad things happen. But they aren't our fault. It's just the way things are."

"You have to remember that he's not rational. His actions prove that."

"Rational or not, he's killing people because of something he thinks Greg and I did. It doesn't feel good, Tony."

"Of course it doesn't. But it means we've got a clue. You've met this person before. It might be in the dim and distant past, but you and Greg crossed paths with him."

She tried to think of anyone from the past who might be the GameMaster but she'd been down this road before. No one had come to mind then, and she was still drawing a blank.

"I just can't think who it could be," she told Tony.

"Maybe it'll come to you later," he suggested.

Dani wasn't so sure. If she'd crossed paths with someone like the GameMaster, surely she'd remember it.

When they got back to headquarters, they were met on the ground floor by an ashen-faced Battle.

"I need you in IT," he said. "There's another one."

"Another one, guv?" Dani asked as they went up the stairs.

"On the website. Another video feed. I've got a team ready to go and a second on standby in case he pulls the same stunt he did before."

Dani felt her muscles tighten as adrenaline

coursed through her body. The video feeds brought with them a sense of dread and a terrible anticipation.

Battle took them to Toombs' office, where the technician was in his usual seat. The laptop was open and the website showed a new square with a timer that was already at *4:00.14*

"Four minutes," Dani said, feeling the adrenaline surge increase. "He isn't giving us much time."

"We're ready to mobilise," Battle said. "And everyone has been briefed to look for anything at the scene that could help the victims out of whatever situation we find. He left them before, so he might do it again."

An image flashed though Dani's mind: Ian Radcliffe going straight to the lever that opened the water tank.

"Except this time, he probably won't," said Tony. "He knows we're expecting it now, so he'll change it up. He wants to keep us on our toes."

Dani watched the timer count down above the blank square. What face from her past was going to appear there? What new horror had the Game-Master dreamt up?

The timer was down to two minutes now.

A title appeared beneath the timer.

The camper van

"Does that mean anything to you, Dani?" Tony asked.

She shook her head. "Nothing."

Battle let out a breath. "We'll find out what it means soon enough."

Dani's phone buzzed. The screen simply said, *Unknown Number*.

She felt a sudden tremble in her fingers. "I think this might be him."

"Put it on speaker," Battle said.

She hit the speaker button and answered the call.

"Detective Summers," the computer-altered voice said. "This is the GameMaster speaking. In a moment, an image will appear of a camper van. Someone is trapped inside. Your colleagues can deal with that. You have another part to play. I've sent a coordinate to your phone. I could tell you to come alone, but I know you'd never do that. Bring your psychologist friend. You might need a shrink when you see what I've left you."

The line went dead.

The phone buzzed again and a text message appeared with map coordinates. A screenshot of a map, showing the destination as a red pin, also appeared.

"It's in the moors," she said.

The timer reached *0:00.00*

The square on the website expanded to show a camper van sitting in a field on a clifftop. The camper van sat alone. There were no other vehicles or signs of movement behind the curtained windows.

A sign on a fence in the distance read, *Sunnyside Clifftop Campsite*.

Toombs went to work on his keyboard. "The Sunnyside Clifftop Campsite is near Whitby."

"Send me the coordinates," Battle said. He turned to Dani and Tony. "You two, get to the moors. Stay in radio contact. And take Ryan with you. He's upstairs. This could be a trap, so you could do with some extra firepower, if you know what I mean."

Dani nodded. She knew exactly what the DCI meant. Ryan was armed.

"Got it, guv."

She and Tony left Toombs' office and went upstairs to the main floor. Ryan was sitting on the edge of an empty desk. He wore a black bomber jacket, black T-shirt, blue jeans and boots over his wiry frame.

When he saw Dani and Tony, he slid off the desk, grinning.

"Looks like the band's back together."

Dani had to admit she was glad to see him. He may have lied to everyone about working for MI5, but his strength and no-nonsense attitude was something they needed at the moment.

Like Battle had said, this journey to the moors could be a trap. Tom Ryan might have deceived them about his role in the secret service, but Dani trusted him to protect her and Tony.

"Come on," she said. "We're taking a trip to the moors."

"Ooh, nice. Are we taking sandwiches?"

"No, but you're bringing your gun."

He raised his eyebrows. "Sounds intriguing."

"We'll brief you on the way."

They went downstairs and out to the car park, where Dani and Tony got into the Land Rover while Ryan fetched his gun from the boot of his Aston Martin. A minute later, he was climbing into the backseat of the Land Rover, the weapon concealed beneath his jacket.

A number of vehicles were leaving the car park, sirens blaring and lights flashing. Battle had obviously decided to eschew the stealthy approach this time. It meant the press would be hot on his heels, but probably didn't care about that; his only focus would be the person trapped inside the camper van.

Dani had large scale maps of the moors—a holdover from when she was investigating the Snow Killer—in the glove compartment. She asked Tony to hand them to her and she checked them against the coordinates on her phone.

The location the GameMaster was sending them to was a remote section of moorland. The nearest road was three miles away.

"We'll park here, at this gate, and proceed the rest of the way on foot." She pointed out the location on the map to Tony and Ryan.

"Sounds good," Ryan said. "Now, does someone want to tell me what's going on?"

Tony filled Ryan in as they left the city behind and headed towards the moors.

Dani's radio crackled and Toombs' voice said, "Just to let you guys know, another video feed has appeared on the website. I can see moorland, but nothing else."

Whatever was going to happen at the location he was sending them to, the GameMaster obviously deemed it worthy of being captured on film.

"Who is this maniac, Doc?" Ryan said from the backseat. "You must have a theory in that massive brain of yours."

"I don't know," Tony said, shaking his head. "He seems to identity with a young boy whose family is dead. I think he suffered a similar tragedy at a young age and blames Dani and her old partner for it."

"Her *dead* old partner," Ryan said.

"Yes."

"Do you have a security detail protecting you, guv?" the MI5 agent asked Dani.

"No," she said, looking at Ryan in the rearview mirror.

He pursed his lips. "Seems to me this nutter might want to do the same thing to you as he did to your old partner."

The thought had already crossed Dani's mind. She hadn't been sleeping well lately.

"Do you think this is a trap?" she said.

"Yeah, it could be. Sending you out onto the moors while everyone else is busy at some campsite. It could very well be a trap."

When they reached the roads that cut through the moors, the radio crackled again.

"Umm, guys," Toombs said. "I can see you."

"What do you mean?" Dani said.

"A smaller, inset window has appeared over the view of the moors and I can see your Land Rover driving along the road. It's shot from above. Must be a drone."

Ryan turned around in his seat and looked up at the sky through the back window. "Yeah, it's a drone. I can see it."

"How many people are watching this, Chris?" Tony asked.

"More than half a million," came the reply.

The psychologist sighed. "They're probably hoping to see some sort of spectacle involving death. Nothing has changed since the days of the Roman arenas."

"Well, we won't give them what they want, will we?" Ryan said. "We're going to come out of this unscathed."

"Chris, what's happening with the camper van?" Dani asked.

"Everyone's still *en route*, including an armed response unit. Battle isn't taking any chances."

She wondered who was trapped in the camper van on the cliff. Someone she knew? Someone she'd helped in the past?

She shouldn't divert her focus. She had to trust Battle to do his job while she focussed on the moors.

They arrived at the old gate on the map and got out of the Land Rover. Dani looked up and saw the drone hovering overhead. She had half a mind to get Ryan to shoot the bloody thing out of the sky.

"It's that way," she said, pointing at the bleak moors. Although the sun was shining and the sky cloudless, the landscape ahead of them looked cold and desolate. A strong wind blew from the North, agitating the grass and heather.

The gate was chained and padlocked, so they climbed over it one by one and made their way across the moors. The drone followed, whirring incessantly.

Battle gritted his teeth as he drove towards Whitby. In front and behind him, the police car sirens wailed and lights flashed. In the rearview mirror, he could see the black van that the FSU—Force Support Unit—team were in. He wasn't taking any chances; when he got to that camper van, he wanted to be prepared for anything.

He was damned if he was going to let the Game-Master get one over on him again.

He keyed his radio. "Toombs, what's happening?"

"Nothing so far, boss. The camper van is just sitting there."

"What about Summers?"

"She's making her way over the moors with Ryan and the doc."

"Keep me informed if anything changes." In the distance, he could see Whitby, the fishing town that inspired Bram Stoker to write *Dracula*. High on the East Cliff, the ruins of the abbey loomed over the harbour.

Sunnyside Campsite was situated north of the town, on the rugged coastline.

The convoy of police and emergency vehicles turned in that direction before reaching Whitby and soon arrived at their destination.

A large sign read, *Sunnyside Clifftop Camping*. And beneath that, *Closed Until Further Notice*.

As he got out of his car, Battle thought it odd that the campsite was closed at the time of year when it must do most of its business. It wasn't as if it was closed for refurbishments or anything like that; the place consisted of nothing more than a field.

Now that he was standing at the fence that marked the campsite's boundary, he could see the camper van in the field. The grass was overgrown, yet there were no visible tyre tracks cutting through it; the camper van had been here for some time.

Carmichael, who was in charge of the FSU came over to Battle. "Shall we send the drone in to have a look before we go barging in there?"

Battle nodded. "Try and have a look through the windows. I want to know what's inside before we send our men in."

Carmichael nodded and waved his arm at one of the black-suited FSU officers. The drone lifted up into the air and angled across the field towards the camper van.

The airborne unit descended and hovered near the windows.

"They're painted black, sir," the drone operator said. "I can't get a visual on anything inside."

"All right, bring her back." Carmichael directed his attention to Battle. "You want me to send my men in?"

Battle leaned on the fence, considering his next move. They knew the cabins at the Sutton Forest Campsite had been wired to explode, so who was to say the camper van wasn't a similar trap?

Except at Sutton Forest, the cabins had been the wrong choice. Being blown up had been the Game-Master's idea of punishment for choosing wrongly.

Here, there wasn't any choice. No cryptic sign telling them to choose wisely. There was just the camper van.

He let out a long breath. What if they did nothing? They only had the GameMaster's word that someone was trapped inside, and Battle trusted that not at all.

The radio in the Range Rover crackled and Toombs' voice said something Battle couldn't hear. He opened the car door and leaned in, snatching up the radio. "Say again, Toombs. I didn't get that."

"There's a camera inside the camper van," the

technician said. "Another window has opened up and I can see someone in there."

"Tell me what you see."

"A woman. She's lying on the floor."

"Is she alive?"

"I can't tell. She's not moving."

Battle had no choice now. He had a responsibility to the person inside the camper van.

"Carmichael," he shouted to the FSU officer. "Get a team in there. There's a woman lying on the floor."

Carmichael nodded and gathered four of his men together. He had a quick word with them, and then they were climbing over the fence one by one and assembling on the other side.

Carmichael came over to the Range Rover. "Don't worry, we'll get her out safe and sound."

Battle looked towards the field, where the four black-suited, helmeted officers were proceeding through the long grass in single file to the camper van.

Carmichael raised a radio to his mouth and said, "Talk to me, Blue Leader, over."

"This is Blue Leader. No signs of life. About to make entry. Checking door."

Battle saw the lead officer reach for the camper van door and try it. He tensed, half-expecting an explosion.

The door swung open.

"Ready to make entry on your signal," Blue Leader said.

Carmichael looked at Battle for confirmation. Realising he had no choice, Battle nodded.

"Go, go, go," Carmichael said into the radio.

Battle heard Blue Leader shout, "Armed police! We're coming in!" and then the four men slipped inside the camper van.

"Talk to me," Carmichael said into the radio. "What do you see?"

"Female on floor. Checking for vital signs." There was a pause, then Blue Leader said. "Is this supposed to be a joke? It's a mannequin."

"Get them out of there," Battle said, feeling a sudden hollowness in his gut.

The camper van door swung shut.

"What the hell?" Blue Leader said.

Battle heard the camper van's engine turn over and then roar into life.

"Get out of there," Carmichael shouted into the radio.

"The door's locked."

The camper van's engine revved and the vehicle began to move forward, towards the edge of the cliff.

Carmichael was shouting into the radio again. "Blue Leader, exit the vehicle by any means possible."

"There's no way out." A hint of panic had crept into Blue Leader's voice.

The camper van picked up speed.

"Turn the engine off," Carmichael said. "Put the handbrake on."

"Negative. There's no handbrake. All the controls have been stripped out. There isn't even a steering wheel."

Carmichael vaulted over the fence and sprinted through the long grass towards the runaway vehicle, even though there was nothing he could do to stop it.

The camper van reached the edge of the cliff and went over.

Battle found himself climbing over the fence, joined by other officers and paramedics.

A growing feeling of dread overtook him as he crossed the field and when he reached the edge of the cliff and looked down at the mangled vehicle on the rocks hundreds of feet below, he knew there couldn't possibly be any survivors.

"Get a rescue team down there," he told the nearest officer. "Get the Coast Guard if you have to."

He turned away, afraid that any rescue attempt would be in vain.

That fear was confirmed when an explosion ripped through the air from the rocks below the cliff.

There were no survivors.

The GameMaster had made sure of that.

———

CHAPTER SEVENTEEN

Dani, Tony, and Ryan finally reached the location on the map. There were a few trees here, but nothing else, as far as Dani could see.

"What are we looking for?" Ryan asked.

She shrugged. "I have no idea."

Her phone rang. *Unknown Number*

She answered it and said, "We're here."

"I know you're there, Detective. I can see you, and so can half a million people. They are going to witness the moment when you realise your efforts in the Snow Killer case were futile. You may have caught the killer, but was anybody saved?"

A sudden, sinking feeling made Dani feel sick. She had saved someone from the Snow Killer. Kate Lumley.

"This didn't turn out exactly as I'd planned," the voice in her ear said. "Even I couldn't get a pool of ice to remain frozen outdoors in this weather. So, I used my ingenuity and came up with something just as good."

"What have you done?" Dani said in a weak voice. At the mention of ice, her mind had become filled with images of the girls who had been found on the moors. The Snow Killer's victims. Each one frozen in ice, with a red ribbon in her hair.

"Behind the tree to your left is a hollow in the ground," the Game Master said. He hung up.

With trembling legs, Dani approached the tree and saw the place where the ground dipped in to a hollow.

Don't let it be Kate, she recited over and over in her mind. *Don't let it be Kate.*

When she stood on the edge of the hollow, her worst fears were realised. Kate Lumley lay in the natural depression. Her body had been encased in clear resin—the GameMaster's substitute for ice—and a red ribbon had been tied into her hair.

CHAPTER
EIGHTEEN

"You can't go home tonight," Ryan told Dani. "Not without some sort of security measures in place."

He was pacing near the fence while Dani sat on the back seat of the Land Rover, the door open.

The road around them—which had been deserted earlier—was now busy with emergency vehicles. A dozen uniformed officers and a SOCO team were trudging over the moors to recover Kate Lumley's resin-encased body and examine the scene.

Dani had a blanket over her shoulders—courtesy of a paramedic from the ambulance that was parked by the gate—but still felt cold. She couldn't stop shivering.

"I have to go home," she told Ryan. "I've got to look after my dogs."

"I thought your neighbours did that if you weren't there."

It was true that Dani had an agreement with her

neighbours that if she didn't arrive home in the evening, they went around to her cottage and fed Barney and Jack but she didn't want to rely on Elsie and Bob if she could help it.

Besides, the real reason she wanted to go home wasn't only because of the dogs. She didn't want to live her life in fear.

If she stayed away from the cottage, or changed her life in any way because of the GameMaster, then he'd won.

"You can stay in a hotel for a couple of nights," Ryan said. "I'll arrange a security detail."

"No," she said.

"Just a couple of nights."

"What happens after that? As soon as I go back home, I'm in the same danger. The only way I can be safe is if the GameMaster is stopped."

"That could take some time."

"Yes, it could. And I can't spend that time looking over my shoulder every minute of every day."

He came closer to the Land Rover and lowered his voice. "Do you know how to use a gun?"

"What? No, I don't need a gun."

"All I'm saying is, I can get you a revolver. Simple to use. You might not even need it, but if you *do*, it's there."

"If I killed the GameMaster, I'd go to prison for murder. Who would look after my dogs then?"

He smiled tightly. "All right, I can see I'm not going to convince you to have a gun, but at least let me watch your place tonight. I'll park on the road outside, just to keep an eye on you."

"I'm sure the DCI will arrange something. Let him work out the personnel and the shifts. There's no need for you to stay up all night."

He sighed. "All right, guv."

She wasn't sure if she *was* his guv'nor anymore, considering the fact that he technically worked for MI5, but at least he seemed to respect her authority.

Tony came over and looked at her with concern in his eyes. "How are you, Dani?"

"I've been better."

"If you need anyone to talk to, you know where I am."

"Thanks, Tony."

"Did you hear what happened at the camper van?"

She could tell by the tone of his voice that it wasn't anything good.

"We lost four of the FSU team," he continued.

"Did he rig the camper van?" Ryan asked.

The psychologist nodded. "It went over the cliff edge with the men locked inside."

Dani balled her fists angrily beneath the blanket. How many more people were going to die before this ended?

"The GameMaster might have inadvertently given us a lead," Tony said. "The camper van was at a campsite that was mysteriously closed, and the place where he left David was near an old campsite in the forest. Two campsites. It might mean something. I've got the support team looking into who owns them."

"Let's hope it leads to something," Dani said. She doubted the GameMaster would do anything that might lead them to him, but she had to hold onto any scrap of hope.

Tony's phone rang. He answered it, walking over to the gate to speak to whoever was on the line. The call was short. Tony nodded and put the phone back in his pocket.

"Thomas Rayburn," he said, walking back to the Land Rover. "Apparently, he's the owner of both the Sunnyside campsite and the Sutton Forest one, as well. There's a connection."

"Could he be the GameMaster?" Dani said.

"I doubt it. He's 74 years old."

Dani's radio crackled and Battle's voice said, "Summers, are you there? Over."

She reached through the gap between the seats and answered it. "Here, guv."

"I heard what happened. I'm sorry. Who's there with you?"

"Ryan and Sheridan, guv."

"Good. I want you to go home. You've been through enough today."

"But, guv—"

"No arguments. Take Ryan with you. He can make sure you're safe until I can sort out a security roster."

She sighed. There was no point arguing with the DCI. "All right, guv."

"Put Sheridan on."

She handed the radio to Tony.

"Here, Boss," the psychologist said.

"I want you back in the office. Grab a lift with one of the uniforms. You need to work up a profile of the so-called GameMaster. You must have enough to go on by now."

"Actually, I was going to have a word with a Thomas Rayburn."

"Who the hell is that?"

"He owns the campsite where the camper van was, and the campsite near where we found David."

There was a pause, then Battle said, "All right. Take a uniform with you. Then get back to the office."

"Got it, Boss."

"And Summers," Battle said, "I want you to go home right now. Try to get some rest. Over and out."

Tony put the radio back into its cradle. "Well, there you go. We've got our orders." He looked at the police cars parked along the edge of the moor. "I need to find someone to give me a lift."

"See ya later, doc," Ryan said.

Tony nodded. "Yeah, see you later. Try to get some rest, Dani." He walked away, in search of a uniformed officer to take him to Thomas Rayburn's house.

"Like the doc said, we've got our orders," Ryan said.

Dani nodded, sighing. She really didn't want to

go home. She needed to be part of the investigation, not sitting on the sidelines.

"If you want to prolong the process, we can go and get my car from HQ first."

"All right, let's do that." She pushed the blanket from her shoulders and started to get out of the backseat.

"You stay there," Ryan said. "I'll drive."

"Ryan, I'm fine."

"I know. That's why you can drive home from HQ when we pick up my car. But until then, you need to take it easy."

"You know I could order you to let me drive, right?"

"You could, but you won't." He slipped into the driver's seat and adjusted the mirrors.

"Don't worry," he told her. "I drove plenty of Land Rovers when I was in the Regiment. I'll get us there without a scratch. Buckle up."

She sat back in the seat and put the seatbelt on. Ryan's reassurances were redundant; she trusted him to drive her car.

He started the engine and pulled onto the road. "I hope you've got something to eat at your place. I'm starving."

———

Tony found a police car with a uniformed officer behind the wheel, seemingly doing nothing.

He tapped on the passenger side window.

The officer—who was a Sikh man in his thirties with a black turban instead of a police helmet on his head—buzzed the window down.

"Can I help you, Doctor?"

"Are you doing much at the moment?"

The officer shook his head. "I was called up here, but everything seems to be in hand. I was just about to go back to the station."

"I need you to come with me to question a suspect."

The officer's eyes lit up. "Certainly. Jump in." He unlocked the door and Tony got in.

"I'm officer Badwal, Doctor. You can call me Ram. It's short for Ramandeep."

"And you can call me Tony."

Ram nodded. "All right, Tony. Where are we going?"

"Hedgemoor House, near Sutton-on-the-Forest. We're going to speak to a man named Thomas Rayburn."

He showed Ram the address the Support Team had texted him and the officer typed it into his onboard computer.

When he was satisfied that he knew their destination, Ram started the car and they set off.

"So, why is Mr Rayburn a suspect?" he asked.

"He owns the campsite near where we found David and the one where the camper van was parked."

Ram nodded solemnly. "I heard about what happened. Very bad news."

"Rayburn is 74, so I doubt he's the man behind all this," Tony said, "but he's connected to both locations, so we need to have a word with him."

The officer nodded. "Understood."

They drove in silence for a few minutes, then Ram said, "I saw you on the front page of the papers this morning. He indicated a folded copy of *The Sun* that was sitting on the dash.

Tony picked it up and unfolded it. The picture on the front page was taken from the website feed. It showed him pulling David out of the ground. The headline read, *Hero Psychologist Rescues Boy From Killer*.

Tony folded the paper and put it back where he'd found it.

"It says you caught a serial killer in Canada," Ram said.

"It wasn't just me. I was working with the Ontario Police Department." That wasn't strictly true, though. The police had no leads. It had been Tony who'd bumped into Solomon Gantz at a petrol station and recognised him as the Lake Erie Ripper.

Ram looked a little disappointed at Tony's playing down of the situation. "But you saved two girls," he said.

"Yes, I did do that," Tony agreed.

"That must be a great feeling. To know that two people are alive today because of you."

"I'm just glad I got there in time." The timing of his arrival at Solomon Gantz's house had been fortuitous for the two girls he'd saved, but for ages afterwards, he'd beaten himself up mentally for not getting there sooner. How many victims might have been saved if he'd bumped into Gantz two days earlier? Or a month earlier?

Those types of thoughts could send the mind down paths of self-doubt and depression, and had been part of the reason Tony had ended up in a mental health facility.

They found Hedgemoor House—a detached, two-story building in its own acre of land—on the outskirts of Sutton-on-the-Forest. Ram took the police car up the drive and parked behind a green BMW that was sitting in front of the house.

"I'll do the talking," Tony said. "If you could take notes, that would be great."

"Of course," Ram said.

They got out of the car, and the uniformed officer got his notebook ready.

Tony knocked on the front door. He heard sounds within the house and fished his Murder Force ID out of his pocket.

The man who answered the door was tall but stooped over. He had thinning white hair and a weathered face that spoke of decades spent outdoors in all weathers. His clothes—a green knitted jumper and black trousers—seemed to hang from his wiry frame.

"Yes?" he said when he saw Tony.

"Mr Rayburn?"

The man nodded.

"I'm Dr Sheridan and this is PC Badwal. We'd like to talk to you about your campsites."

Rayburn nodded. "I wondered when the police would show up. I didn't expect a doctor, though."

"I'm a psychologist," Tony explained.

"Hang on, aren't you the bloke in the papers? The one who saved that boy?"

"Yes," Tony said. "May we come in?"

"Of course." He stepped back into the hallway and shouted, "Jo, put the kettle on. The police are here."

He led Tony and Ram through the house to a kitchen at the rear, where a woman in her fifties was filling a kettle at the sink. She wore jeans and a white blouse.

"This is my daughter Jo," Rayburn said. "She comes round most days to make sure I'm still alive and kicking."

"Don't be silly, Dad," she said, "You'll outlive us all." She smiled at Tony and Ram. "Take a seat and the tea will be ready in a minute."

"Thanks." Tony took a seat at a pine table that was situated beneath a large window. Beyond the window, a large, colourful garden was in bloom. Ram took a seat next to him and placed the notebook on the table.

"I assume you're aware of what happened at your campsite today," Tony said.

Rayburn, who was leaning on the kitchen counter, nodded. "Hell of a thing."

"Do you know anything about the camper van?"

"No. I saw it there a few times. It's been there for over a month. But I never went near it."

"You didn't wonder why it was there? I noticed the campsite was closed."

"Not so much closed as privately rented," Rayburn said.

"What do you mean by that?"

Rayburn looked uncomfortable. "When I explain this to you, it's going to sound a bit dodgy, but I can assure you that I had no idea what he wanted it for. I didn't know he was going to…do what he did."

"Perhaps you'd better start at the beginning," Tony suggested.

"Sit down, Dad, and I'll bring you a cuppa over," Jo said. "Tell them about the money."

Rayburn took a seat at the table across from Tony and Ram. "The money appeared two months ago. And when I say appeared, I mean it was left on the doorstep in a brown envelope. A fat wad of cash."

"Nearly a hundred grand," Jo said, pouring the tea.

"With a note," Rayburn added, "asking me to close Sunnyside until further notice. The note said a camper van would be situated on the site and the owner wanted privacy."

"And you didn't think it strange?" Tony asked.

Rayburn shrugged. "Well, of course I did, but the hundred grand was more than I'd have made from keeping the site open for the season, so I was willing to overlook any strangeness."

"Have you still got the note?"

"Yeah, it's here somewhere."

"It's in the drawer," Jo said. She brought three mugs of tea over the table, along with milk and sugar, before opening a drawer and taking out a small piece of paper which she handed to Tony.

He took it by the edge and placed it on the table in front of him. The message had been typed on a computer and printed out.

Tommy, I have enclosed a substantial fee for the sole use of Sunnyside campsite. Please close the campsite until further notice. I will be using the site for my camper van and I require absolute privacy. The enclosed money should more than cover any losses incurred from being closed.

Make your day great!

J.

Tony reread the ending sentiment. *Make your day great!* didn't sound like the GameMaster at all.

"This is a rather friendly tone," he said. "Do you know the person who sent it?"

Rayburn shook his head. "I don't think so. But there is something strange about it. I haven't been called Tommy in over ten years. That's what the campers used to call me when I worked on the sites. I employ other people to do all that now, so nobody has called me that since I retired."

Tony frowned at the salutation on the note. "So, this was written by someone who knew you in the past."

"It looks like it, but I don't know anyone with the initial J."

"Maybe you can't remember them, but they seem to have known you at some point."

Rayburn looked suddenly worried.

"Tell me about the Sutton Forest campsite," Tony said. "When did it close down?"

"A long time ago. Must be going on twelve years now. It wasn't bringing in much revenue on account of it's in the middle of nowhere. Campers these days like pubs that serve food. We couldn't do that out there."

"Before you retired, did you work there personally?"

"Sometimes."

"And the campers there knew you as Tommy?"

Rayburn nodded. "It was the name I used when I was on the sites. Sounded more friendly than Thomas."

"You weren't known as Tommy by anyone other than the campers?"

"No. Everybody else calls me Thomas, or Tom. Never Tommy."

Pointing at the note, Tony said, "I'm going to have to take this as evidence."

"Of course."

"You can't think of anyone you met on the sites who might have struck you as odd in some way?"

"Plenty," Rayburn said, "but no one who would do what this maniac's doing."

Tony downed his tea and put his business card on the table. "If you remember anything, please contact me."

"All right, I will."

"Do you have any questions, Ram?"

The uniformed officer consulted his notes. "Just one. Mr Rayburn, you said you saw the camper van at the Sunnyside campsite a number of times."

"That's right. When I was driving past. I'd always have a look because I was curious."

"Did you ever see anyone at the campsite with the vehicle?"

"No, just the van."

"What about other vehicles? Were there any cars parked nearby on the occasions when you saw the camper van?"

Rayburn's brows furrowed. "I'm not sure. I think I might have seen a black car parked by the gate the last time I was driving past. Or was it the time before?" The furrow between his brows deepened. "Or was it both?"

"Do you know the make of the vehicle?" Ram positioned his pen over the notebook.

Rayburn grimaced. "Possibly a Lexus. I can't say for certain."

"Was there anything about the vehicle that would distinguish it from other, similar cars? A scratch on the bodywork, or a dent? Perhaps stickers in the windows?"

"No, nothing like that. I'd remember something like that."

Ram closed the notebook and smiled. "Thank you for your time, Mr Rayburn."

Tony pointed at the note. "Do you have an evidence bag for this?" he asked Ram.

"I can get one from the car."

When the uniformed officer returned with the clear plastic bag, Rayburn said, "There is one more thing. Now that I think about it, I *did* see someone at Sunnyside. But this was before the money and the note arrived. Probably a few weeks before."

"Tell us about it," Tony said.

"I got to the campsite, just to have a look around. The boys had been in with the mowers the day before and I wanted to make sure everything was neat and tidy. I saw this bloke standing at the edge of the cliff, looking down at the rocks."

"Can you describe him?" Tony said.

"I'd say he was in his twenties. Light hair. Well built."

"Did you speak to him?" Ram asked.

"No. I don't think he saw me, to be honest. He was only there for a few seconds, then he walked off."

"You didn't think it strange that he was on your campsite?"

Rayburn shook his head. "The coastal path runs through the campsite, along the top of the cliff. Plenty of people walk along it."

"So why did this man stick out in particular?" Ram asked.

"Well, like I say, I wouldn't have thought anything of it, except he was crying."

"Crying?" Tony said.

"Yeah. Proper sobbing. That's another reason I didn't talk to him. I didn't want to disturb the poor bloke."

"You didn't happen to see the black Lexus parked nearby, did you?" Ram said.

"No. I don't think I saw any other cars parked at the site that day. I assumed this bloke was a hiker."

Ram nodded and wrote in the notebook. "Was he wearing hiking gear?"

Rayburn frowned, trying to remember. "I think so."

"Thanks, Mr Rayburn," Tony said. "You've been very helpful."

He got out of the chair and thanked Jo for the tea.

When he and Ram were outside, with the note safely sealed inside an evidence bag, Tony said, "That was him. The bloke on the cliff was our guy."

"How can you be so sure?" Ram unlocked the car and they both got in.

"I think the man we're looking for has survived some sort of tragedy. The police failed him in some way. He's lashing out, but part of him is distraught over what happened. I think Thomas Rayburn saw that side of him that day on the cliff."

"Shame he didn't go to therapy instead of taking it out on innocent people."

Tony nodded. "And now he's spiralling."

"What does that mean?"

"It means that very soon, he's going to lash out again."

CHAPTER
NINETEEN

Dani parked outside her cottage, followed closely by Ryan in his Aston Martin.

As she got out of the Land Rover, she cast a wary glance at the road and the moors. There were no unknown vehicles sitting in wait. No strangers lurking on the moors near her home.

Ryan climbed out of his sports car and made the same visual checks. Seemingly satisfied, he turned to Dani and said, "All quiet."

Dani slid the key into the front door. Barney and Jack were going crazy inside.

"They're not going to attack me, are they?" Ryan said eyeing the door warily.

It was the first time Dani had seen him be remotely scared of anything. "You'll be fine. You're with me, so they know you're friendly."

She opened the door and the dogs bounded out, tails wagging. They rushed around Ryan in a tight circle, sniffing his legs.

"See?" Dani said. "They like you."

He nodded and followed her inside. The dogs remained close to him.

"What would they do if a stranger got into the house?" he asked.

"To be honest, I don't know. They bark at the postman, and anyone who comes to the door who they don't recognise, but I don't think they'd attack anybody. They're too friendly."

"Oh." Ryan seemed disappointed. "I was hoping they'd be a bit more vicious. It'd be an extra layer of protection."

"Maybe they'd attack someone if they broke in," she said. "Or if I was in danger. I'm sure they'd attack someone who was hurting me."

He nodded, but didn't seem convinced. The dogs were currently wheeling around him, tails thumping on the floor.

"Do you want something to eat?" She opened the fridge, suddenly aware of how little she had in it. "Ready meal?"

"Excellent."

She inspected the labels. "Lasagne, spaghetti bolognese, or cottage pie?"

"Cottage pie sounds great. Thanks."

She put the pie in the microwave and chose a lasagne for herself.

"I'll make a brew," Ryan said.

He filled the kettle at the sink and turned it on. He took two mugs from the mug tree on the counter and opened the cupboard directly above the kettle, guessing correctly where Dani kept the tea bags.

Dani watched him while she waited by the microwave. It was strange to have a man in her kitchen, and making tea, no less. The scene of shared domesticity contrasted so starkly with her usual solitary lifestyle that she felt a sudden sting of loneliness.

The microwave pinged and she took the cottage pie out, using the oven gloves to slide the hot plastic tray onto the counter before putting the lasagne in to heat up.

She squeezed past Ryan and fed the dogs.

While Barney and Jack tucked in, the microwave pinged again. Ryan opened it and used the oven gloves to place the lasagne next to the cottage pie on the counter.

Dani took two plates down from the cupboard and slid the trays onto them. She got a couple of forks from the cutlery drawer and handed one to Ryan, along with a teaspoon.

He used the spoon to take the tea bags out of the mugs and toss them into the bin.

Dani went to the fridge and got the milk. "Sugars in that cupboard there," she said, pointing. She knew he took two sugars in his tea.

When the drinks were made and the cellophane had been removed from the meals, they sat at the small pine table in the corner of the kitchen and ate.

"How are you feeling?" Ryan asked.

"I'm still in shock, I suppose." She felt cold and

hollow, as if someone had scooped her insides out with a spoon, leaving only a shell of who she had once been.

Ryan shovelled a forkful of cottage pie into his mouth. "We won't let him get to you, guv."

She nodded but said nothing. They both knew the GameMaster had seemingly limitless resources. So far, he'd done everything his way. The game had played out exactly as he'd wanted it to. It would be foolish to think things were going to change now.

Everything that was happening right now had been planned by the GameMaster for years. Even though everyone had been unaware of his existence, he'd been working behind the scenes to set everything up just as he'd wanted.

He'd planned Greg's abduction and murder two years ago. Had he been arranging a similar fate for Dani for all these years?

If so, he'd probably accounted for a police security detail. He had a way around it.

"He doesn't care that you're watching me," she said to Ryan. "If he did, he wouldn't have made it obvious that I'm a target by calling me."

"Maybe he slipped up by doing that. Perhaps he couldn't help himself. He might have scuppered his own plans by putting us on high alert."

She shook her head and took a bite of the lasagne. "I don't think so. I think he doesn't care that there's a security detail watching me because he has a way around it."

"Now that's just paranoid."

"I don't think so. You can't watch me forever. Maybe he'll wait until the security is called off, and come for me then. He's been planning this for years, so a few extra weeks is nothing to him."

"I don't think he's going to wait weeks. He struck fast and has been building up momentum. He doesn't want to lose that."

"You sound like Tony. Getting into the mind of the killer. It's a useful technique."

He shrugged. "Until it isn't."

"What do you mean by that?"

"Well, look what happened to the doc. He delved too far into the criminal mind and almost didn't make it back."

"He seems okay now."

"Yeah." He concentrated on eating his meal.

She watched him, trying to figure him out. Was he saying he didn't approve of Tony's methods, or was there more to this?

"Tony told me you helped him when he was having a panic attack."

"Panic attack? I don't remember that."

"Maybe not panic. But he was having an anxiety attack."

"Lots of people don't like hospitals."

"So, you *do* know what I'm talking about."

Ryan shrugged. "He was having problems going inside the hospital in Whitby, so I talked to him. Distracted him. That's all."

"Tony told me it was as if you knew about his problem, even though he hadn't told anyone."

He didn't answer.

"Ryan, did you know?"

He finished the cottage pie and looked at her earnestly. "How could I know that?"

"That's what I'm asking. Have you read files on us? Does the government have a file on me? Are you reporting back to them to add more details?"

He looked shocked. "No, not at all. That really *is* paranoia. The government doesn't have secret files on everyone. If they do, I certainly haven't seen them."

"But you knew about Tony's issue with hospitals."

He sighed. "Yes, I knew."

"How?"

"If I told you that, I'd have to kill you," he said, attempting to lighten the atmosphere.

"Ryan, you're not spying on us, are you?"

"No, I'm not. I swear."

"That's the only way you could know about Tony, as far as I can see."

He paused for a few seconds, seemingly mulling over something. Finally, he said, "All right. I'll tell you. But it stays between us, okay?"

"Okay," she said, intrigued.

"A few years ago, the Canadian and British governments jointly ran a survival training exercise for military personnel in the Canadian wilderness. I was one of the staff, teaching survival techniques and making sure none of the recruits got lost in the wilds.

"Two weeks in, I got a call on the satellite phone from my superiors at Thames House. They wanted me to check on a British national who was in Canada helping the police with a serial killer case."

"Tony," Dani guessed.

Ryan nodded. "Yeah. Tony. I didn't know who he was at the time, of course. Just that he was a British psychologist helping the Canadian police and the powers-that-be in London were interested in him and his work."

"MI5 was interested in Tony? Why?"

"I'll get to that in a minute," he said. "I did as I was asked. I came out of the wilderness, bought some civvy clothes and hired a car. I drove down to Lakeshore, a small town in the area where Tony and the Canadian police were working, and I watched them while they tried to solve the case."

"I still don't understand why MI5 was so interested in Tony."

"Neither did I, at first. Then I found out from a friend in Thames House that it was because they were considering Tony for a case they were working on. A serial killer case."

"So, they wanted to see how well he did with the Lake Erie Ripper before they hired him."

"Yeah. They used the Lake Erie case as a kind of audition. What better way to see if Tony was up to the job than watch him in action?"

"And you were the one watching him and reporting back to your superiors."

Ryan nodded. "At first, it looked like Tony and

the police were getting nowhere fast. Girls were still vanishing. Bodies were still turning up. It didn't look like the Ripper would ever be caught. The guys back in London were swiftly coming to the conclusion that Tony wasn't up to the job. They were about to pull me off the case when Tony broke the case."

"He recognised the Ripper, right?" She'd read about the case in the papers at the time, and had revisited the articles after meeting Tony.

"Yeah. All that time when nothing seemed to be happening and the police were getting nowhere, Tony was building up a psychological profile of the Ripper in his head. He was slowly gathering clues about who this guy was. And when he happened to bump into Solomon Gantz, he recognised him immediately."

"Were you there the night Tony went into the Ripper's house?"

"No. I'd been told to stop my surveillance and get ready to head north again. I was in my hotel room when I heard what had happened. I got over there as quickly as I could, posing as a reporter. Tony wasn't in a good way. He'd been physically injured. While I watched him being driven away in an ambulance, I called Thames House and asked them what I should do next."

"I bet they couldn't wait to get their hands on him."

"At first, yeah. Then it became obvious that Tony's wounds weren't only physical. He had mental scars, as well. As soon as my bosses became aware that he'd been taken to a mental health facility, they wanted nothing more to do with him. They told me to return to the wilderness survival course and forget all about the side mission to Lakeshore."

"That's terrible," Dani said. "They abandoned him because he was no longer useful to them."

"That's how they work. Anyway, I went back to the wilderness but I couldn't stop thinking about Tony. He'd come all the way to this country to help the police catch a murderer and now, he'd been abandoned. Lost in the system. It didn't sit right with me."

"Did you do anything about it?"

"When the course was finished, I took some leave and tracked him down. He was in a psychiatric unit near Toronto. I pretended to be his brother so I could get inside and see him. Talk to the doctors."

"You visited him? Didn't they check who you were?"

"I've worked under aliases before. Pretending to be a relative to get inside a hospital was child's play."

"So, you saw Tony?"

Ryan nodded. "He was heavily sedated, so the doctors didn't think it was strange that he didn't recognise me. I just wanted to check that he was okay. I couldn't bear the thought of him being forgotten by everyone, so far away from home."

Dani scrutinised Ryan's face closely. He was

staring down at the tabletop, but she could tell his thoughts were a million miles away.

"Is that because of something that happened to you?" she guessed out loud.

"Not me. My little brother Dave. He joined the army when he was eighteen. Following in my footsteps. He was on a mission in Kandahar when his squad was captured. We all thought he was dead until an American Navy Seal team broke him and some other soldiers out of a prison compound a year later. He was never the same after that. He told me that the only thing that kept him going was knowing that I was looking for him."

He looked up at Dani with despair in his eyes. "But I wasn't. I'd been told he was dead. Our mum and dad buried an empty coffin and tried to move on. We abandoned him. He needed us, but we didn't even know it."

"And that's why you wanted to make sure Tony was okay?" She'd never seen this side of Ryan before—hadn't even known he had a brother.

"Yeah, maybe. I don't know. I just couldn't abandon him the way I'd abandoned Dave."

"So, that's how you knew about his fear of hospitals. The doctors at the psychiatric unit told you."

He nodded. "He had a bad time in those places. The drugs he was on, combined with the mental trauma he'd suffered, didn't do him any favours. He was having hallucinations, paranoid delusions, you name it. During one of his more lucid moments, he told the staff that being in a hospital was making him worse. So they moved him to a place called Mackenzie House, where patients had their own chalets in the grounds of a Victorian house. That's where he completed his recovery."

"And he had no idea that you'd visited him?"

"No. When they weaned him off the drugs and he became aware of his surroundings, I couldn't visit anymore. He would have blown my cover. I kept in contact with the doctors by email, telling them I was back in England, but I stopped that, as well, when it became obvious Tony was going to make a full recovery."

Dani thought about what she'd just been told and said, "So, it isn't a coincidence that you were sent to join Murder Force. They sent you because you had previous dealings with Tony."

"I don't know how the high-ups at Thames House think, but it's likely, yeah."

"And what's this case they wanted Tony to work on?"

He leaned across the table and lowered his voice. "They think there's a serial killer who's been active in Britain for the past two decades. Doing his dirty work in the shadows. No signature. No tell-tale signs that the murders were committed by the same person. No connection between the victims. He's working entirely behind the scenes unnoticed."

"Except MI5 *has* noticed him."

"Even they're not sure. This guy—if he exists—is like a ghost."

"Doesn't sound like much to go on."

"It isn't, which is why they wanted Tony's help."

"Until he was injured by the Ripper."

"Yeah."

Dani drank her tea, mulling over this new information. When she put the mug down, she said, "Sounds like MI5 want to keep an eye on Murder Force in case we stumble across this serial killer."

"Most likely."

"You're not sure?"

"I'm not. I'm as much in the dark as you are."

She got up and cleared the table, throwing the ready meal containers in the bin and placing the empty mugs in the sink.

Politics and shady goings-on weren't her thing. She preferred straightforward police work. The fact that Murder Force's work was being scrutinised by a government agency left a bitter taste in her mouth.

"Battle has set up a rota," Ryan said, looking at his phone. "There should be someone here in half an hour. Looks like I've got the 3:00 am shift."

"You should get home. Get some sleep."

"Not until the first shift starts. I'm not leaving you alone."

She nodded and washed the mugs. Was this how her life was going to be until the GameMaster was stopped? Never being alone? Always being watched?

Perhaps sensing her unease, Ryan said, "I'm going to check around outside. Do you think you'll be leaving the house at all?"

"I have to walk the dogs."

"Okay. Just tell whichever officer is outside at the time. They'll make sure you're okay."

"You mean they'll follow me over the moors." She couldn't keep the frustration from her voice.

"We want to keep you safe, guv." He went outside, closing the door behind him.

Barney sniffed at the door, as if he wanted to go with Ryan, and Jack whined.

"Don't worry," she told them. "We'll go for a walk in a bit."

She sat in the window seat and watched as Ryan made an inspection of the cottage before returning to his car. He saw her at the window and waved.

Dani waved back. Then she put the telly on and tried to forget about the threat hanging over her life.

A threat so serious that she had to be watched day and night.

CHAPTER
TWENTY

Tony stared at the notebook on the desk in front of him. Despite Battle telling him he must have enough to make a profile by now, the notes offered scant information.

He closed his eyes and tried to put himself in the GameMaster's shoes.

"I'm undoing the good deeds of the past," he mumbled to himself. "I'm killing everyone whose life was saved by Hughes and Summers."

"Is that a confession?" a voice said.

Tony opened his eyes to see Ian Radcliffe sitting at the desk opposite, a grin on his face.

"I'm just trying to get inside this guy's head," Tony explained.

"I see. Would you do it better over a pint? We can brainstorm, if you like."

Tony narrowed his eyes, wondering why the counter terrorism officer would want to go for a drink with him. He voiced his thoughts with a blunt, "Why?"

Radcliffe frowned. "Why what?"

"Why do you want to go for a pint?"

"Why not? We aren't getting anywhere sitting here. A change of scenery will do us the world of good. Give us a fresh perspective."

Tony checked his watch. It was almost knocking off time. Visiting Thomas Rayburn had eaten up most of the afternoon.

And a pint might blow away the mental cobwebs.

"All right," he said. "But just one. My girlfriend goes away tomorrow, and I've booked us a table at Bellini's."

"Very nice." The counter terrorism officer got out of his chair and stretched. "I can only have one myself. I'm on security duty outside DI Summers' house at 1:00 a.m."

"Battle roped you in, did he?"

"I volunteered. We've got to look after our own."

"True," Tony said. "Right, let's go. Where do you have in mind?"

"There's a pub just around the corner. The Anchor. Probably as good as anywhere else."

"I'll see you there," Tony said, casting a glance at Battle's office. The DCI was sitting at his desk, looking at paperwork. "I just need to have a quick word with the boss."

"I'll get the beers in," Radcliffe said, pushing through the door to the stairwell.

Tony knocked on Battle's door. The DCI looked up from the papers on his desk and said, "Have you got something for me, doctor?"

"That's what I'm coming to tell you. I'll have a profile on your desk first thing in the morning. It's been a hectic day. I need to get in the right headspace."

Battle sighed. "All right. But I want some insights into this so-called GameMaster. Something that'll help us catch him. God knows, we need it."

"No problem, boss. I'll see you tomorrow." Tony offered the DCI a brief smile that he hoped was reassuring and returned to his desk, where he picked up his notebook and pen before leaving.

He climbed into his Mini and drove the short distance to the Anchor, where he found Radcliffe waiting for him at a corner table inside the gloomy pub.

"So, what have you got so far?" Radcliffe said as Tony took a seat and set his notebook down.

"Not much, to be honest. The theory I want to explore more—and it's nothing more than a theory at the moment—is that he suffered some sort of tragedy which he blames the police for. More specifically, he blames Greg Hughes and Dani."

"You don't have more than that?"

Tony shook his head and took a sip of the beer Radcliffe had bought for him. "Not really."

"You must have something else. Something useful."

"Are we here to brainstorm? Or for you to tell me I'm not doing my job properly?"

"All right, all right." Radcliffe held up his hands in mock surrender. "I just hoped we'd be closer to catching this guy."

"Don't we all?"

"You really haven't got anything more in that notebook of yours?"

"Well, I know he's got a lot of money and resources."

"That's a given," Radcliffe said. "I thought you might have something less obvious."

"Like what?"

"Like an insight into who he is."

"I told you I didn't have much. I thought that was why we're here. To brainstorm."

"Yeah," Radcliffe said, sipping his pint. He looked disappointed.

"You all right?" Tony asked.

"I'm fine. I just…"

"Hoped we'd be closer to catching him," Tony finished for him. "You said that already."

"Well, it's true."

Tony scrutinised the man sitting opposite him. Radcliffe's disappointment seemed to go deeper than mere frustration at the lack of progress on the case. Tony could sense the man's anxiety rising with each passing second.

"Do you have any thoughts?" he asked, more to gauge Radcliffe's reaction than anything else. There was more going on here than two colleagues brainstorming over a pint.

"He knows people's secrets," Radcliffe said in a low voice.

"What makes you say that?"

"Well, I mean, he knew about all those people that were saved by Di Summers and her partner all those years ago."

"Those events were reported in the media. They weren't secrets."

"No, I suppose they weren't." His eyes went to his pint, concentrating on the mahogany-coloured liquid in the glass.

"Ian, is there something you want to tell me?" Tony asked. He leaned forward over the table slightly, showing the counter terrorism officer that he was attentive and ready to listen. It was a tactic he'd used many times with patients who were unwilling to talk.

"I just mean that someone like him—the GameMaster—can probably hack into anything. Phones. Computers. If he wanted to find something out about someone, he could probably do it."

Tony nodded slowly. "Find out what, exactly?"

Radcliffe shrugged. His eyes never left the pint. It was as if he could see something in the dark liquid that no one else could. A memory, perhaps. "I don't know."

"Secrets?"

Radcliffe gazed into the beer for a few seconds longer, then seemed to snap out of it. He moved his attention to Tony and forced a grin. "Like I said, I don't know. Just brainstorming. That's why we're here, right?"

"It is," Tony said. Whatever Radcliffe had been on the verge of telling him would have to wait for another time. The moment was gone.

"So," Radcliffe said, "tell me any theory you might have, no matter how ridiculous it might be. You must have something. Let's hear it."

Tony did indeed have a few theories and ideas. He knew the GameMaster had some connection to the Sunnyside and Sutton Forest campsites. He'd probably visited them more than a decade ago, when Thomas Rayburn was known to the campers as Tommy.

But he said none of that. Instead, he downed his pint and made a point of looking at his watch. "I'd best get going, Ian. We'll catch up tomorrow in the office."

Radcliffe's face fell. "But I thought we were going to throw some ideas around. We might have a breakthrough. We might work out who he is."

"Look, I've got to give Battle a profile tomorrow morning. You can have a read of that and if you can think of anything to add to it, let me know."

Radcliffe's head dropped to his chest and shook slowly. "Tomorrow morning will be too late."

"What?" Tony wasn't sure if he'd heard the man correctly. Radcliffe was mumbling.

The counter terrorism officer let out a long sigh. "Nothing. It doesn't matter."

"Right. I've got to go, but if you want to talk, give me a call. Anytime. Okay?"

"Yeah. Okay."

If Tony had the slightest hope that Radcliffe would open up about what was troubling him, he'd stay and talk to the man, but he knew the counter terrorism officer wasn't going to say anything more than he already had, and that was hardly anything at all.

Tony also had a gut feeling that he shouldn't tell Radcliffe anything about his thoughts on the GameMaster. Radcliffe seemed…compromised…in some way. He certainly knew more than he was letting on.

"See you tomorrow," he said.

Radcliffe nodded but didn't lift his head. "Yeah."

Tony left the pub and got into his car. He was going to have to mention this to Battle in the morning when he delivered the profile. There was something going on with Radcliffe. Maybe the DCI could get to the bottom of it.

He tried to put it out of his head as he drove across town to his flat, but the conversation stuck with him for the entire journey. What had Radcliffe meant when he mentioned secrets? And there was something else about the conversation that niggled at Tony's mind. Something he couldn't quite put his finger on.

When he got home, Alina came out of the bedroom in a figure-hugging black dress.

"Wow," Tony said. "You look stunning."

She grinned and twirled around. "Thank you, kind sir."

"Looks like I'm going to have to go to some effort now," he joked.

She narrowed her eyes and thumped him playfully on the shoulder. "How was your day?"

"Not great," he said. "I suppose it was on the news."

"Yes," she said, her expression becoming serious. "It's terrible what happened to that poor woman."

He nodded. "I'm going to have a shower and get changed. I'm going to try and forget about work, at least for tonight."

He went into the bathroom and turned the shower on. Stepping into the hot spray, he tried to clear his mind and become present in the moment. He was going to have a lovely meal with his beautiful girlfriend at one of the top restaurants in the city. Work could wait until tomorrow.

He'd get into the office early and put together a profile for Battle, no matter how scant it might be.

It was only hours later—in the dead of night, when he was lying awake in bed with Alina sleeping soundly next to him—that Tony realised what had niggled him about the conversation with Radcliffe.

"GameMaster," he said, sitting up in bed. "Radcliffe said GameMaster."

Battle had insisted that the name go no further when they'd heard it in on the video message from the GameMaster. Only a handful of people knew the name, and Radcliffe was not one of them.

"Radcliffe has been contacted by the GameMaster," he mumbled into the darkness. "That's how he knows the name. He's been in contact with him and he never mentioned it."

Other pieces of his conversation with Radcliffe replayed in his memory.

Tomorrow morning will be too late.

I'm on security duty outside DI Summers' house at 1:00 a.m.

Tony looked at the clock on the bedside table. The glowing red numerals said, *1:22.*

Radcliffe was outside Dani's house right now.

He picked up his phone and called her. The call rang and rang and then went to voicemail.

"Dani, call me back," he said after the beep. "Radcliffe has been lying to us and he's outside your house."

Alina woke up. "Tony? What's the matter?"

"There's a problem." He was already dialling Tom Ryan's number.

Ryan picked up after two rings. "Doc?"

"Listen," Tony said. "There's something off with Radcliffe. I think he's been contacted by the GameMaster. And he's outside Dani's house right now."

"Have you warned her?"

"I've tried calling her but there's no answer."

"I'm on my way." Ryan hung up.

"Tony, what's happening?" Alina put a hand on his shoulder.

"Dani's in trouble. I've got to get over there." He slid out of bed and searched for his clothes.

"She knew the GameMaster would find a way through the security detail, and she was right. He's had a man on the inside all this time."

CHAPTER
TWENTY-ONE

Tom Ryan gritted his teeth as he sped towards Dani's house. It was almost half past one. Anything could have happened in the last thirty minutes.

His phone rang. He pressed the button on the steering wheel to answer it.

The voice that filled the car was Battle's. "Dr Sheridan just rang me and filled me in. How far are you from her house?"

"Fifteen minutes, sir."

"I'll get some uniforms over there." There was a pause and then the DCI added, "Bring Radcliffe in for questioning. Don't do anything stupid. I want him in custody, not dead. Understood?"

Since the moment he'd left his flat, Ryan had considered a thousand things he'd like to do to Radcliffe, but he knew the DCI was right. They needed the man alive. He had information.

"Is that understood, Ryan?" Battle repeated.

"Yes, sir."

"Right. I'm on my way over there, but contact me the second you have anything to report." The DCI hung up.

Ryan put his foot down. He was already taking a risk, speeding along the winding, narrow roads in the dark, but it was a risk he was willing to take. If anything happened to Dani, he'd never forgive himself.

He should have realised there was a mole in the department. The guy they were after didn't leave anything to chance. He'd want someone on the inside, reporting back to him on the state of the investigation. He'd use that information to execute his plans.

How could Ryan have missed it? Granted, he'd only been back on the Force a couple of days, and had barely interacted with Radcliffe at all, but he should have guessed that the man was compromised.

He knew that was irrational. There was no way he could have known about Radcliffe. But he needed to distract himself from the thoughts of what he might find when he got to Dani's cottage, and mentally berating himself was all he had.

He tried ringing Dani's number, but there was no answer. He knew there was no way she'd turn her phone off at night. It would be next to her on the bedside table. He couldn't allow himself to entertain his dark thoughts regarding the reasons why that phone wasn't being answered.

Thirteen minutes later, he sped through the

village of Tollby and saw blue lights flashing in the distance. The uniforms were already here.

As he got closer, he saw two police cars parked on the road outside Dani's cottage. He parked next to them and got out of the car. His gun was in a shoulder holster, snug against his body and hidden beneath his jacket.

The cottage door was open and a uniformed constable was standing outside it. When he saw Ryan, he raised his hand. "You can't come in here, sir."

"Yes, I can," Ryan said, flashing his Murder Force ID at the man. "What's the situation?" He stepped inside the house. The first thing he saw was Dani's dogs. They were lying on the rug, on their sides, tongues lolling out of their mouths.

Two male officers and a female officer were in the house, flashing torches over the walls and floor as they inspected the place.

Ryan turned the lights on. "Is she here? Is DI Summers here?"

The female officer shook her head at him. "We've only just got here, but it looks like she's gone. There are signs of a struggle in the bedroom. We think the dogs have been drugged. The vet's on the way."

Ryan pushed past them to the bedroom. The bedside table was on its side, a lamp, clock, and Dani's phone on the floor.

"Did you see any vehicles on your way here? Vehicles driving away from the house?"

She thought for a moment. "We only saw one other car. These roads are quiet at this time of night."

"Where?"

"We were coming from Whitby direction. It was going the opposite way."

"Towards Whitby?"

She nodded.

Ryan ran out of the house and got in his car. As he started the engine, he rang Battle.

"What is it?" the DCI said, trepidation weakening his voice.

"She's been taken." Ryan put the car into gear and accelerated away from the cottage. "I think Radcliffe is heading towards Whitby."

"Whitby? Why would he go there?"

"The beach," Ryan said grimly. "Greg Hughes' body was found on a beach, wasn't it?"

There was silence on the other end of the line for a few seconds, then Battle said, "Get her back, Ryan. By any means possible."

"Got it." He took the turning for Whitby and pressed the accelerator as far as he dared on these roads.

Battle had hung up.

Ryan gripped the steering wheel tightly and sped along the road that cut through the dark, lonely moors.

―――

It took him much too long to get to Whitby and, as he drove into the coastal town, he feared the worst for Dani. He had no idea how far ahead of him Radcliffe had been. Despite the speed with which Ryan had driven over the moors, Radcliffe could have had time to do anything by now.

He drove along Pier Road, which skirted the harbour, and brought the Aston Martin to a halt at the top of a wide, cement ramp that led down to the beach.

As he exited the car, his hand slid automatically beneath his jacket and slid the Glock out of the shoulder holster.

He sprinted down the ramp and stopped when he hit the sand, scanning the beach for movement.

The sand shone silver and wet in the moonlight. The tide was receding, the waves whispering over pebbles.

Ryan saw a dark shape in the distance, on the edge of the surf. He wasn't sure if it was a rock, or a person on their knees. Pointing the muzzle of the gun down, he approached warily.

As his night vision improved and he got closer, he realised it *was* a person. Kneeling at the edge of the beach, looking out over the sea.

When he was a few feet away, he saw that it was Ian Radcliffe. The counter terrorism officer was dressed in a black jacket, combat trousers, and boots. He didn't seem to notice Ryan. His attention was focussed on the dark horizon.

"Radcliffe," Ryan said, raising the gun.

Radcliffe turned to face him. When he saw the gun, he raised his hands.

"Where is she?" Ryan said.

"Gone." Ryan could see tears staining the man's cheeks. A sense of despair was evident in his face and the hunched posture of his body.

"Gone where?"

Radcliffe shrugged.

Ryan moved forward, pressing the muzzle of the Glock against Radcliffe's forehead. "Where the fuck is she?"

The counter terrorism officer flinched and pointed out to sea. "Out there. He took her by boat. That's all I know."

Ryan looked out over the waves. There was no sign of a boat out there. There was nothing but blackness.

"He made me do it," Radcliffe said weakly.

"I don't give a fuck."

"Look. This explains everything." Radcliffe reached into his jacket pocket.

Ryan tensed. If a weapon came out of that pocket, he'd make sure Radcliffe regretted the day he was born.

Radcliffe's hand reappeared with something small and black held between the forefinger and thumb. A flash drive. He offered it to Ryan.

Ryan took it, slipped it into his own pocket and then—his anger boiling over—punched Radcliffe square in the face.

The counter terrorism officer collapsed onto the sand, his nose bloody.

Ryan stared out over the dark sea, feeling a sense of hopelessness.

Dani was gone.

CHAPTER
TWENTY-TWO

Toombs' office seemed unusually bright to Tony. He'd spent the past hour driving around in the dark. First to Dani's house, and then to headquarters after being informed that Ryan had apprehended Radcliffe and was bringing him in.

Now that he was here, standing beneath the bright ceiling lights, everything in the office seemed to glare at him. He understood that his mind was playing tricks on him. That he was in shock, and nothing in here was any brighter than usual.

Battle and Ryan were also in the office, both of them looking grim as Toombs slid the flash drive into the laptop.

Radcliffe was in an interrogation room downstairs. They wanted to question him, but needed to see the contents of the flash drive he'd given to Ryan first, in case it contained information that would lead them to the GameMaster.

Now that the GameMaster had Dani, time was quickly running out.

"There's just one file," Toombs said, clicking on the contents of the flash drive. "A video."

Battle leaned closer to the screen. "Let's see it."

Toombs clicked on the file and a video opened. It began to play, showing the inside of a large warehouse. The GameMaster's voice came from behind the camera.

"Ian Radcliffe, this is the GameMaster speaking. For too long, you have been living with a secret. A secret that—if it got out—would ruin you and your family."

The camera panned to the right, revealing a cork board on the wall. Several photographs were pinned to the board. The camera zoomed in on a photo of a young woman with dark hair sitting alone outside a café. She wore sunglasses and a summer dress. The faces of the other café customers had been blurred out, making the woman the centre of attention.

"This is Maria Kozlova, a Russian terrorist responsible for the murder of twelve civilians in Marais, Paris four years ago. But you already know that, don't you, Ian? You had a relationship with this woman during the year leading up to the attack. Does your wife know? Does the anti-terrorism department know? Have they taken a deep dive into your phone and seen the call logs and messages? I dived in, Ian, and it wasn't a pretty sight. You knew about the Marais attack before it even happened and you did nothing to stop it. Was that because you believed you loved this woman, or was it because of the two hundred thousand

pounds that were deposited into your bank two days before the attack?"

"Bloody hell," Battle muttered.

The camera pulled away from the photograph of Maria Kozlova and focussed on a different photo, this one of a man in his fifties with a grey beard.

"This is Grisha Volkov the man who sent Maria to meet you. His terrorist group needed a man on the inside of British counter terrorism. Your department was working closely with French authorities to bring down the group after a number of foiled attacks on British and French soil. You believed you loved Maria, but you were nothing more than a fly caught in a honey trap."

The camera panned across the board to a photo of Radcliffe's family. They were on a beach, beneath a bright blue sky. Radcliffe had his arm around his wife, and his two children—a boy and a girl—stood in the foreground, grinning at the camera.

"What would happen to your family if this secret got out? How would Cindy cope with you behind bars? What would little Charlie and Faith think of their father? How long before they moved on and tried to forget you while you rotted in prison?"

The camera moved again, this time moving away from the cork board and panning around the warehouse to a table, upon which sat stacks of money.

"This can be all yours, Ian, along with your freedom. Certain events will take place soon and I need you to work for me from the inside. After all, you've done it before. This time, the reward won't be sex. It will be your freedom and

your family. Keep the enclosed phone with you at all times. I'll be in touch."

The video ended.

"Go back," Battle told Toombs. "To where the camera moves towards the money on the table."

The computer technician used the timeline to scrub to the point where the camera panned across the warehouse.

"There," the DCI said. "Stop."

Tony squinted at the paused image. As the camera had panned to the left, it had captured the Perspex tank that would later become the method of murdering Frank Moseley.

At the time the video had been made, the tank had been under construction. Wires trailed from its base to the lever that would later be fixed to the wall, but was currently lying on the floor.

"That's how Radcliffe knew about the lever," Battle said. "He'd seen it on this video."

He let out a long breath and said, "Right, we need to question Radcliffe. We also need to have a look at this phone the GameMaster sent to him."

"He had a phone on him when I brought him in," Ryan said.

"Toombs, see what you can do with it." The DCI turned his attention to Tony and Ryan. "Do you two want first crack at him?"

They both nodded.

Battle's expression became grim. "I don't need to tell you what our priority is here."

"Of course not, sir," Ryan said.

"We'll get it out of him," Tony said, more to reassure himself than anything else. They *had* to find Dani. He couldn't allow himself to consider any other outcome.

"I'll have a team on standby," the DCI said. "They'll be ready to move anywhere."

Tony and Ryan left the office and went downstairs to the interview rooms. These rooms were a new addition to the building and had been built in the basement, along with holding cells and an evidence lockup.

Radcliffe was in Interview Room 3, handcuffed to an iron bar that was fixed to the table. When Tony and Ryan entered, he looked up at them with a grief-stricken expression. His nose had been bandaged and his left eye was beginning to swell.

Tony sat opposite Radcliffe. Ryan leaned against the wall in the corner, arms folded.

"I'm going to come right out with it," Tony said. "You're in a lot of trouble, Ian. If you want to make it any easier on yourself, you need to tell us where Dani is right now."

"I don't know." Radcliffe sounded like he had a cold, thanks to his bandaged nose. "I really don't."

"You said she was taken by boat."

Radcliffe nodded.

"Taken where?"

"I'm telling you, I don't know."

Tony felt frustration building inside him. He took a couple of deep breaths to regain control of his emotions.

"We've seen the video the GameMaster sent you. I assume all that is true? About you and the Russian terrorist?"

Radcliffe's head dropped. He nodded. "It's true."

"So, to prevent your little secret getting out, you spied on us and reported back to the GameMaster." Tony didn't phrase it as a question. It was a simple statement of fact.

"I had to. He was going to expose me, otherwise."

"And what did you tell him regarding the case?"

"Nothing, really. I told him what leads were being followed, what connections were being made regarding Greg Hughes, and if he was in any danger of being caught."

"That isn't nothing," Ryan said from the corner.

"Yes, it is. The case wasn't going anywhere. There was barely anything to tell him."

"During your communication with him, did he ever give you any indication of who he was?" asked Tony.

Radcliffe shook his head. "No."

"When he put Dani on his boat, did you see him?"

"He was wearing a balaclava. He stayed in the shadows."

"So, you have no idea what he looks like?"

"It was dark. Listen, if I knew who he was, I'd tell you. It's too late for me, now. The damage is done. I just wish I hadn't handed DI Summers over to him."

"Oh, you've suddenly got a conscience, have you?" Ryan said, moving over to the table and leaning on it with both hands. "If you want to make things right, help us find Dani."

"I want to. Really, I do. But I told you, I don't know anything." His eyes became sorrowful. "Look, I didn't want to do this. That's why I was hoping you'd found out more about him. If there was any chance of catching him, I wouldn't have taken DI Summers."

"So, that's why you grilled me at the pub?" Tony said.

"I wanted to know if we had a chance of getting him. When I realised we didn't, I had no choice. I had to do what he'd told me to. Otherwise, my life was over."

"It's over now, anyway," Ryan reminded him.

Radcliffe nodded. "I know that. I've got nothing to lose by telling you the truth. I don't have a reason to lie. If I knew who the GameMaster was, I'd tell you. You have to believe that, at least."

Tony sat back in his chair and scrutinised Radcliffe. The man appeared honest enough. His body language and expressions weren't guarded. He didn't hesitate when speaking, and his voice didn't waver. He looked like a man who had lost everything and was trying to atone for his sins.

"When he spoke to you, did he tell you his motive?"

"No."

"Don't answer straight away. Think about it for a

moment. Did he say anything that revealed details about himself? No matter how insignificant you think it might be."

Radcliffe went quiet. His bloodshot eyes looked upward, and Tony knew the man was sifting through his memories.

He waited, giving Radcliffe time to process his interactions with the GameMaster.

Ryan went back to the corner and folded his arms again.

"There *is* something," Radcliffe said, finally. "Although it might not mean much."

"What is it?" Tony said.

"He rang me in the middle of the night, once. He sounded upset about something. It was the only time I heard him express any emotion."

"Tell us everything," Tony said. "From the beginning."

"The phone rang at one in the morning. It woke Cindy up as well, but I told her it was work and took the phone downstairs to the kitchen."

"The same phone that he always contacted you on?" Tony asked.

"Yes. When I answered, he sounded upset. He might also have been drunk. I don't know. He was slurring his words a lot."

"What did he say?"

"He said he was going to make them pay and they would all be sorry. I asked him who he was talking about and he seemed to come to his senses a bit. He told me I'd better not screw up his plans.

That I had to do exactly what he told me to do. I said of course I would, for the sake of my family."

Radcliffe looked up at Tony. "It's what he said next that was so out of character. He said, 'At least you've *got* a family' and hung up."

"So, he hasn't got a family," Ryan said. "My heart bleeds. Plenty of people haven't got families, but they don't go on killing sprees because of it."

"Except the GameMaster blames the police for the loss of his family," Tony said. "More specifically, he blames Dani and Greg. And he wants revenge."

He thought about the nature of the crimes committed by the GameMaster. People were being killed in the same manner they would have died if not for the intervention of Dani and Greg Hughes in the past.

It was as if the GameMaster was saying those people should not have been saved. As far as he was concerned, he was putting things right.

But why did he think those people didn't deserve to be saved?

The answer came to him immediately. "He doesn't have a family," he said, "because Summers and Hughes failed to save them in some way. He's lashing out. If they couldn't save his family, then he's going to make sure they couldn't save anyone else either."

"Makes sense in a sick kind of way," Ryan said grimly.

Tony nodded. "It makes complete sense to the

GameMaster. He thinks the death of his family justifies what he's doing."

Ryan pursed his lips. "Like I said. Sick."

Tony got out of the chair and motioned for Ryan to follow him.

They left the room and Tony said, "If we can find the GameMaster's family somewhere in the Summers and Hughes cases, we should be able to figure out who he is. If we know *who* he is, we should be able to find out *where* he is."

"And that will lead us to Dani."

"Hopefully."

They ascended the stairs to the Murder Force offices. Battle was coming down the stairs. "Come with me. Something new has happened on the website."

They followed the DCI to the IT department and entered Toombs' office. The computer technician was looking at the laptop with a grave expression on his face.

When he saw them enter his office, he rolled his chair away so they could see the screen.

A new square had appeared on the *Will the police save them?* website.

The stark, white title over the square read, *Detective in Danger*.

The timer—which simply displayed hours and minutes this time, not seconds—had already begun to count down. At the moment, it was at *07:57*.

Less than eight hours before Dani's live feed began.

CHAPTER
TWENTY-THREE

When Dani woke up, she was in complete darkness. Her head throbbed and her thoughts were muddled. The last thing she remembered was going to bed. Wherever she was now, it was not her bedroom. How had she got here?

She moved slightly and heard bedsprings creak beneath her. She realised she was lying on a thin mattress on a metal bed.

She sat up, and pain flared in her head. Her arms and legs ached. And when she rubbed her right shoulder, where the skin felt tender, as if she'd bumped it into something, she found that she was fully dressed.

She'd gone to bed in her pyjamas. Someone had dressed her.

Dani noticed a tiny red light far above her head. A camera. Watching her.

"Where am I?" she croaked. Her throat was dry, her voice weak.

She heard a *click*, and then a male voice came through speakers somewhere in the room. *"Detective Summers, welcome to your atonement."*

"I haven't got anything to atone for. At least, not where you're concerned."

"That's where you're wrong. You and your partner killed my family."

She shook her head, and instantly regretted it when pain flared in her skull. "We didn't kill anyone. Tell me why you think we did."

"All in good time. Although time is something you are rapidly running out of. The timer is already counting down."

Dani looked up at the red light. "Tell me why I'm here. Why are you doing this?"

"All will be revealed soon, detective."

Another *click* and a timer high up on the wall flashed into life. The glowing red digits cast an eerie glow around the room.

07:43

As Dani watched, the numbers changed.

07:42

The red glow from the timer barely illuminated her surroundings, but it was sufficient to reveal what she'd already guessed. She was in a small, featureless cell. The only items in here were the bed she was sitting on and a toilet in the corner.

Was this where Greg had been brought after he'd been taken? Had he watched that same timer count down the last moments of his life?

Dani refused to believe that this was the end. She wasn't going to go out like this.

If the GameMaster thought he was going to kill her easily, he was mistaken.

She was going to fight tooth and nail to survive.

CHAPTER
TWENTY-FOUR

06:29

Tony hovered around his desk. He had too much pent-up energy to sit down. The clock on the wall drew his eyes every few seconds.

Five-thirty a.m. At twelve noon, the live feed on the website would begin, and Dani would die.

That gave them six and a half hours to work out who the GameMaster was and get to Dani.

"What are you thinking, doc?" Ryan appeared and perched on the edge of Tony's desk.

"I'm thinking there isn't enough time," Tony said frustratedly.

"The Support Team are looking through the old Summers and Hughes case reports, right? Maybe something will turn up."

"They haven't found anything so far, and we're running out of time."

"What about Hughes' widow? Perhaps she knows something."

"It's worth a shot." Tony grabbed his phone and rang Helen Hughes."

"Hello?" Tony had expected Mrs Hughes to sound sleepy, but she seemed to be wide awake.

"Mrs Hughes, it's Tony Sheridan from the police. I'm sorry to ring you so early—"

"That's all right. I don't sleep very well lately, so I'm always up early. Have you found something? It must be important for you to ring at this hour."

"It is important, yes. I was wondering if Greg ever mentioned a case regarding a family tragedy."

"Well, yes. He dealt with a lot of those over the course of his career."

"Yes, of course. More specifically, then, this would be a tragedy where a male member of the family survived. Possibly a young boy."

"Oh, I see. Well, I'll have to think about it."

Tony looked at the clock. "Yes, of course. If you could get back to me the moment you think of something, that would be great."

He knew better than to tell her that Dani's life was at stake. Such stress could hinder the woman's attempts to recall anything, or, worse, cause her to subconsciously create a false memory rather than come up empty handed.

"All right," she said. "Do you have any more details? It isn't much to go on."

"I'm afraid I don't," he said.

"I'll have a look though the scrapbooks."

"Scrapbooks?"

"Yes, I kept clippings of every news story Greg was mentioned in. I assume that what you're talking about would have been in the papers."

"Yes, it would. Mrs Hughes, do you mind if we come over to your house? We could help you look."

"Yes, of course. I'll put the kettle on."

"It'll take us an hour to get there."

"All right, I'll wait."

"See you soon." Tony ended the call and looked at Ryan. "She's got scrapbooks of all the old cases."

Ryan nodded. "I'll drive."

CHAPTER
TWENTY-FIVE

05:32

They pulled up outside the house in Flanders Road and got out of the Aston Martin. Tony tried to stop looking at his watch every few seconds. They had five and a half hours to save Dani. Time was slipping away.

Helen Hughes opened the front door and Tony gave her a brief smile. "This is DC Ryan," he said.

She ushered them into the house. "I'll get the kettle on. The scrapbooks are in the living room."

Tony led Ryan into the living room, where four large scrapbooks sat on the coffee table. One of them was open to a page where a number of newspaper clippings had been glued neatly next to each other.

Tony picked up one of the closed books and Ryan

did the same. They sat next to each other on the sofa and began turning the pages, scanning the headlines.

As well as newspaper clippings relating to Greg Hughes' career, the pages of the scrapbooks were filled with recipes, interior design magazine articles, and pressed flowers.

Mrs Hughes came in and placed a tray on the table. "I'll be mother," she said, pouring tea from the pot into three China teacups. "Help yourselves to milk and sugar."

"That's wonderful, Mrs Hughes. Thank you." Ryan took a cup and added two sugars to it, along with a splash of milk.

Tony did likewise, sipping the hot tea while he balanced the scrapbook on his lap. He turned the page and was faced with a headline that read, *SCARBOROUGH MAN KILLS FAMILY*.

Tony checked the date in the corner of the newspaper clipping. Twelve years ago.

The photo that accompanied the article was a low resolution black and white picture of family on a beach. Five faces grinned at the camera. A dark-haired man wearing shorts and a short-sleeved shirt, a blonde woman in a sun dress and large straw hat, and three children. Two boys and a girl. All three children were fair-haired. The girl looked four or five years old. The youngest of the three siblings. The oldest brother looked fourteen or fifteen, the middle child around twelve.

Tony shifted his attention to the words printed on the page and read them carefully.

Scarborough man, Ronald Graves (42) killed his family and himself yesterday by driving a campervan over the edge of a cliff near Whitby. According to eyewitnesses, the incident was not an accident.

His wife, Fiona (38), daughter Maddy (4), and son Stephen (15) were killed. The family's other son, Jason (12), was injured at the scene and is currently recovering in hospital.

"Mrs Hughes," Tony said. "Why is this clipping in here? It doesn't mention Greg at all."

"Let me have a look, dear."

He passed the scrapbook to her. She squinted at the newspaper article.

"Oh, this," she said. "Greg insisted on keeping that. Said it was a reminder that he couldn't help everyone, no matter how hard he tried." She shook her head slowly. "Such a tragedy."

"Why that particular story?" Tony asked. "Why did that remind him he couldn't help everyone?"

"Greg and Dani arrested Ronald Graves the day before this happened. Domestic disturbance, I think it was. They took him to the station and locked him up for the night, but his wife decided she wasn't going to press charges, so they had to release Ronald the next day."

She looked down at the newspaper clipping and tutted. "Then he went and did this. Terrible."

"And the son who survived," Tony said. "Jason Graves. Do you know what happened to him?"

"He recovered from his injuries. A small mercy, considering he lost his entire family."

"It's him," Tony said to Ryan. "Read it."

Ryan took the scrapbook from Mrs Hughes and read it quickly. "Yeah, it's got to be him."

Tony pulled his phone out of his pocket and called the Support Team at headquarters. As soon as someone answered, he said, "This is Doctor Sheridan. I need to know the whereabouts of a Jason Graves, age 24, from Scarborough."

"Yes, doctor," said the female voice on the other end of the line. "I'll ring you back with the information."

Tony hung up and called Battle.

"What have you found?" the DCI said when he answered.

"Jason Graves. Dani and Greg arrested his father twelve years ago on some sort of domestic disturbance charge, but he was released the next day. He drove his family over a cliff in a campervan."

"Bloody hell."

"Jason survived. The Support Team are trying to locate him."

"How sure are you that it's him, doctor?"

"I'm sure," Tony said. "Jason Graves is the GameMaster."

CHAPTER
TWENTY-SIX

12 Years Ago

Jason dawdled home from school. Carrying his book bag over his shoulder, he ambled along the streets that led to his house, wishing he could be going anywhere else in the world.

He'd even considered running away a couple of times, but he was only twelve, and he had no idea where he would go, or how to take care of himself. He didn't even have any relatives he could stay with. His mum was an only child and her parents—Jason's grandma and grandad—had both died when Jason was a baby.

His dad was adopted and didn't get on with his parents. No surprise there. His dad didn't get on with anybody.

So that meant Jason only had Stephen and

Maddy. And his mum, of course. Maybe when Stephen was old enough to leave home, he'd take Jason with him.

That sounded like a fantastic idea, but the more Jason thought about it, the more he realised it would never happen. He couldn't leave his mum and Maddy at home with his dad. He could never do that. Besides, Stephen was only 15, so it would be at least three years before he was old enough to leave, and that seemed like an eternity to Jason.

When his house came into view, he stopped on the pavement and let out a long sigh. There was no getting away from it. No matter how much he wished things were different, that house was his home and he had to live there.

As he pushed through the gate and walked up the path to the front door, he felt his shoulders hunch and his head drop. It was as if he was trying to make himself smaller. Less noticeable.

He opened the front door and went inside.

The first thing he did when he entered the house was try to figure out where his father was. He stood in the hallway and sniffed the air, trying to detect the origin of the cigarette smoke that hung in the air.

It seemed to be coming from the living room. The telly was on in there and Jason could hear what sounded like the news. His dad's favourite pastime to watch the news and complain. He blamed the news for everything. Said the world was going down the toilet.

CHAPTER TWENTY-SIX

Jason quietly put his book bag down and walked quickly past the open living room door. His mum was in the kitchen. He could hear her talking to Maddy. And the smell of spaghetti sauce drifted from that direction. Much better than cigarette smoke.

"Jason, is that you?"

Jason froze when he heard the voice coming from the living room. He wanted to run to the kitchen, away from the cloying smoke and the gravelly voice.

"Yes," he said weakly. He hoped that was the end of the conversation. That his dad would go back to watching the telly and complaining about the price of petrol or something.

"Come here."

Jason swallowed and slowly turned to face the living room doorway. He didn't want to go in there, but he knew that if he didn't do what his dad told him to, he'd be sorry.

He took a single step through the doorway but went no further. His father was slouched on the settee, wearing only a dirty vest and jeans. It didn't look like he'd been to work today. He'd stayed home quite a lot lately, preferring to watch telly and drink than go to his job at the paint factory.

An ashtray was balanced precariously on the arm of the settee, overflowing with cigarette butts. Empty beer bottles were piled up on the carpet.

"Get me another beer." His dad didn't even look at him. His eyes were glued to the telly.

Jason nodded and went to the kitchen. His mum was in there, standing by the oven, making spaghetti. Maddy was roaming around with a doll in each hand.

"Jason!" his mum said, grinning when she saw him. "How was school?"

He shrugged. "Okay." He went to the fridge and said, "Dad wants another beer."

Her face became worried. "Oh."

Jason took a bottle from the fridge and took it to the living room. His dad was lighting another cigarette.

Jason handed him the beer.

His dad took the bottle and gestured at the telly with it. "Those miners in New Zealand have died. Just because those blokes were rescued in Chile last month, the New Zealand authorities thought they'd get these miners out as well. But they didn't. An explosion killed all of 'em. Their time was up, and that was that. They'll never learn. You can't rescue everybody."

He looked up at Jason and sneered. "I don't know why I'm telling you any of this. You're too young to understand."

Jason said nothing. He understood a lot. His teachers had called him gifted. That was something his dad didn't know, because Mum had kept it from him at Jason's request. No need to give this bitter alcoholic a reason to single him out for punishment and ridicule.

He slipped out of the room and went to the kitchen. "Where's Stephen?"

"He's staying at his friend's house tonight," said Mum.

Jason sighed. He wished he could stay at a friend's house. But the truth was that, even though he had friends, he never asked to stay at their houses, or even go for tea. Because then they'd expect him to reciprocate, and he could never do that. He couldn't bring a friend here. Not when his father was around.

He noticed his mum's hand shaking as she stirred the bolognese sauce in the saucepan. He knew she was scared about what was going to happen later. When Dad drank like this, he liked to argue. And fight. He lashed out with his fists.

Jason wished there was a camping trip to look forward to. In the Summer holidays, his mum always took him, Stephen, and Maddy camping. Dad never came. He couldn't be bothered. So the four of them had a wonderful time.

Camping trips were Jason's favourite things in the world. And he knew they were his mum's as well. She saved up most of the money she made at her job in Asda to hire a camper van and buy everything they needed for their week away.

Everyone was friendly at the campsites they stayed at. And Tommy, the man who ran them, was always telling bad jokes, which made Jason laugh even though they were terrible.

But it was ages before they'd be going camping

again. It was November now, which meant there were eight months to go before their next getaway.

Mum dished out spaghetti for Jason and Maddy. They sat at the kitchen table and started eating.

"Do you want spaghetti, Ron?" Mum waited a few seconds for an answer and, when none, came, brought her own bowl over to the table.

Jason rarely saw his father eat these days. The man seemed to exist on beer alone.

"When you've eaten, you'd best go up to your room to do your homework," Mum said to Jason.

He nodded. She was giving him an excuse to get out of the way for when the shouting started later.

"And you can go to bed early as well, young lady," she said to Maddy.

Maddy nodded, and that made Jason feel sad. Most four-year-olds would fight to stay up, but his sister wanted to get out of the way of their father and would gladly go to bed to do so.

Jason finished his spaghetti and said, "I'll go up and do my homework, then." He only had a bit of maths and a couple of English questions to do. He found those subjects easy. It shouldn't take him more than ten minutes to do the work.

Then, he planned to play games on his computer. He and his friends usually played World of Warcraft together, talking to each other through headsets while they raided dungeons.

Jason loved killing monsters, and his character was a high-level Death Knight who didn't take any nonsense from anyone. His answer to problems was to kill his enemies. If only the real world was as simple, Jason thought as he grabbed his book bag from the hall and went upstairs.

When he got into his room, he closed the door and threw the book bag on the bed. Homework could wait for now. He'd see if any of his friends were online.

He sat at his desk and booted up the computer. When he logged into the game, he found that Derek, his friend from school, was online. Derek's online handle was GameGeek. That was nowhere near as cool as Jason's name.

He put his headset on and heard Derek's voice immediately. "Hey, Jason, are you there?"

"Don't call me Jason, GameGeek. We only use our online names on here, remember?"

"Sorry," Derek said. "I forgot."

Jason shifted slightly in the chair and tried to get into character, imagining himself as a powerful Death Knight who killed everyone who got in his way.

When he felt he'd achieved the proper mindset, he grinned and said, "This is the GameMaster speaking."

CHAPTER
TWENTY-SEVEN

12 Years Ago

A noise downstairs woke Jason. Or perhaps he'd just dreamt it. He wasn't sure, so he slid out of bed and crept to the door in the darkness. He opened it quietly.

The landing was dark, but the lights were on downstairs. His father was down there, shouting.

"No one appreciates what I do for this family!"

Although there was no reply, Jason knew his mother was down there as well, and the shouts were being aimed at her.

It was at this point that Stephen would usually appear from his bedroom and tell Jason to go back to bed. That there was nothing they could do. He'd tell Maddy the same thing, if she was awake. But

CHAPTER TWENTY-SEVEN

Maddy seemed to be asleep in her room and Stephen wasn't here.

So, Jason crept to the top of the stairs.

The next noise he heard was a slapping sound followed by a whimper. That second sound had come from his mum.

Jason felt angry and scared. Why did they have to live with this terrible man? Was it going to be like this forever? What if his dad hit his mum so hard that he killed her?

Jason couldn't imagine a world in which his mother was dead. A world in which he and his siblings had to live with just their father.

Before he knew what he was doing, he was on the stairs, going down them quickly to the hallway.

The shouting and other noises were still coming from the kitchen as he went to the phone that was mounted on the wall and picked up the receiver.

The dial tone buzzed in his ear.

He dialled 999.

"Emergency. Which service?"

"Police," Jason said. He felt a hot tear run down his cheek.

There was a *click*, and then a female voice said, "Police. What's your emergency?"

"My dad is hitting my mum."

"Is this happening right now?"

"Yes. They're in the kitchen."

"What's your name, sweetheart?"

"Jason. Jason Graves."

"Can you tell me your address, Jason?"

"Yes." He told her the address.

"All right. I'm sending a car over there right now. Is there somewhere safe you can go until the officers arrive?"

"My bedroom."

"Can you stay on the phone with me while you're in your bedroom?"

"No. The phone is in the hallway."

"All right, sweetheart. You put the phone down and go to your room. The officers are on their way. They're almost there."

"Okay." Jason replaced the receiver and crept back upstairs to his room, where he sat on his bed in the dark.

Downstairs, the shouting continued until there was a loud knock on the front door.

Jason's father stopped mid-shout and then mumbled. "Who the hell is that?"

Jason felt a tightness in his chest. Maybe he shouldn't have called the police. He didn't want to make things worse. What had he been thinking?

He knew the answer to that, of course. He'd been hoping the police would take his father away. Put him in jail. But now they were actually here, he wasn't so sure that was really going to happen.

He heard the front door open and his dad say, "What do you want?"

Then other, quieter, voices drifted up from downstairs, but Jason couldn't hear what they were saying. He went out onto the landing and peered over the railing.

What he saw filled his heart with joy. His father was being led out of the front door in handcuffs by a policeman.

A uniformed policewoman was talking to Jason's mum, trying to calm her down.

"Mum?" Jason said, going downstairs.

His mum looked up at him. Tears streaked her face. "Jason, go back to bed."

"What's happening?" he said. He knew what he hoped was happening, but he needed to hear it from a grown up. Was his dad really going to jail, like he deserved?

"I said go back to bed!"

He froze on the stairs. He thought his mum would be happy. Their dad was gone. They didn't have to be scared of him anymore. Didn't have to tip toe around him as if he were a sleeping bear they were desperate not to wake up.

The policewoman turned to him and smiled. "Hi, Jason. I'm PC Dani Summers. You go back to bed and your mum will be up to see you in a minute, okay?"

No, it wasn't okay. He didn't want to go back to bed. He wanted to know if his family was really free of the bear. Instead of going back upstairs, he ran outside in his pyjamas.

"Jason! Get back here!" his mother called after him.

The police car was parked by the kerb, and his dad was in the backseat, looking sorry for himself.

The policeman who'd taken his dad away in cuffs

was standing by the car, probably waiting for his partner. When he saw Jason, he crouched down so they were eye-to-eye.

"Hey, there. You'd better go back inside. It's cold out here."

Jason didn't even feel the cold. His heart was hammering in his chest and he felt hot. "I don't want to go back inside. I want to know how long you're going to put him in jail for."

The policeman smiled. "We don't put people in jail. That's up to the courts. Are you Jason?"

Jason nodded.

The policemen lowered his voice. "You did a very brave thing when you rang us, Jason."

"I needed you to come and save my mum."

"Well, we've done that. Don't worry, your dad won't be coming back tonight."

From the backseat of the police car, his dad saw him and shouted. "Jason! Jason, tell them I didn't do anything!"

"You go back inside now," the policeman said.

The policewoman—Dani—was coming out of the house. "I've got a statement, Greg," she said to her partner, "but Mrs Graves is obviously upset at the moment. Might be best to come back tomorrow when she's calmed down."

Greg nodded. "Okay. We'll do that." He looked at Jason and said, "You've done all you can tonight, Jason. Leave the rest to us."

"But I want to know—"

"Jason!" his mother shouted from the front door. "Get back inside. Now. You'll catch your death!"

He sighed and went back up the drive. No one listened to him because he was a kid. He couldn't wait until he was older. He'd make sure everyone listened to what he had to say. He wouldn't be ignored anymore.

When he got inside, his mum closed the front door. "Jason, I want you to be honest with me. Did you call the police?"

He nodded.

A look of despair came over her. "Why? Why would you do that?"

"So they can save us."

"They can't save us, Jason."

"They can. I've seen it on telly."

"This isn't telly. This is real life." She paced the hallway, clenching and unclenching her hands. "We're going to have to leave. When your father gets out, he'll be furious. He could do anything."

"Maybe he won't get out. The police—"

"The police can't save us, Jason."

Jason felt his chest hitch. Hot tears filled his eyes. He'd thought he was doing the right thing by calling the police, but he'd just made everything worse.

"Don't cry," his mother said. "Go and pack your suitcase. Put everything in that you would if we were going on holiday. In fact, that's what we'll do. We'll go on holiday. I'll ring the hire company in the morning and see if we can have the campervan for a week. Your dad might have calmed down by then. Or maybe two weeks."

His mum was rambling, so Jason quietly went upstairs and got his suitcase from the back of his wardrobe. He opened it on the bed and took some clothes and underwear from his chest of drawers.

He wasn't sure how he felt about going away on a camping trip tomorrow. He'd wished for that very thing earlier, but now he wasn't so sure it was a good idea. Going on holiday when his mum was so upset might somehow sully the memory of all the good times they'd had in the past.

After packing the case with everything he needed —clothes, books, and a couple of toys—he placed it on the floor and lay on the bed, staring at the ceiling. He wished he hadn't called the police. He'd made everything worse.

His mum might tell Maddy and Stephen they were going on holiday but Jason knew the truth; they were running away.

———

By late afternoon of the next day, they were on the road. His mum had managed to get the campervan for a week, and they'd picked Stephen up from his friend's house.

Stephen had been surprised to see the campervan, but hadn't questioned it. Jason got the feeling that Stephen knew something had gone wrong at home and that they were now on the run, like fugitives.

Mum was smiling and pretending nothing was wrong, but Jason knew she was just putting on a brave face. He could see the anguish behind her eyes.

"Are we going to see Tommy?" Maddy asked. She was sitting next to Jason in the backseat. Stephen was in the front seat, next to their mum.

"Not this time," Mum said. "The campsites are closed at this time of year."

Maddy frowned. "Where will we stay, then?"

"We'll find somewhere."

Jason sighed. This was no holiday. If they couldn't stay at one of the campsites, they'd end up in a field in the middle of nowhere, or in a car park somewhere. That wasn't fun. And even if they went to the beach, it was too cold to go in the sea.

After what seemed like forever, they left the main road and rumbled along a narrow, gravelly road that led to the cliffs.

"Who's hungry?" Mum asked.

"Me!" Maddy said.

"All right. We'll stop by the sea and have something to eat."

"Where are we sleeping tonight?" Jason said.

"In the campervan."

"Yes, I know that. But *where*? If we can't stay at a campsite, where *will* we stay?"

"We'll find somewhere."

He sighed again. His mum had obviously not

planned this out properly.

Jason liked to plan everything, where possible. Making plans and sticking to them made him feel in control of his life.

Half an hour later, the campervan was parked in a field, by the top of the cliffs. Mum was inside, making sandwiches with Maddy while Jason and Stephen wandered to the cliff edge to have a look at the beach below and work out if they could climb down to it.

"What's going on?" Stephen asked when they were out of earshot of their mum.

"Dad was hurting Mum last night, so I called the police." Even saying it made Jason feel embarrassed, but he had to tell his brother the truth. It wasn't fair for Stephen to be dragged out on this false holiday and not know why.

"What were you thinking? You've made everything worse."

"I know. I didn't mean to. I just wanted someone to help us."

They reached the edge of the cliff. It was obvious they weren't going to be able to climb down to the beach below. The tide was in. The sea crashed on the rocks at the base of the cliff.

"The police can't help us," Stephen said. "No one can. And when they release Dad, he's going to go ballistic."

"They can't release him," Jason insisted. "He's a bad man."

"And you think that makes a difference to them? The police let bad people go all the time. Did you think they were knights riding around saving people or something?" Stephen snorted derisively.

Jason said nothing. That was *exactly* what he'd thought. Dani and her partner Greg had seemed like nice people. Like *good* people. Surely, if anyone was going to save his family, it was them.

"You need to become part of the real world," Stephen said. "All that gaming is warping your sense of reality."

Jason didn't have an argument or comeback, so he just looked at the ground, shrugged, and said, "Whatever."

"I'm going to help Mum," Stephen said before marching away to the campervan.

Jason didn't feel like going back, so he wandered along the clifftop, mulling over the events of last night. Despite what Stephen said, there was no way the police would let their dad go. They had to know how bad that would make things for everyone.

If they released his dad, then they were just as bad as he was. The smiles and kindness that had been shown to him by Dani and Greg was nothing but a lie.

He had to believe that his mum and Stephen were wrong. The police *could* help. They *could* save his family.

He saw a man and woman coming towards him

along the clifftop. They wore thick jackets and rucksacks and poked walking poles into the ground with every step as they followed the coastal path.

As they passed him, they both smiled and said, "Hello."

Jason raised a hand in greeting.

He watched them as they passed the campervan and continued on their way. Why couldn't his dad be friendly and smiley like that man?

A car on the gravelly road caught his attention, and his blood froze when he recognised it. It was their car. The red Ford Mondeo that his mum did the shopping in every week. The car that his dad always complained about.

And his dad was behind the wheel.

Jason felt rooted to the spot. He watched as the car skidded across the grass and came to a stop beside the campervan.

His father got out and slammed the car door.

At the same moment, his mum appeared in the campervan doorway and said, "Ron, what are you doing here?"

"Get inside. Now. We're going home!" He pushed her into the vehicle and followed, closing the door behind him.

Jason heard muffled voices inside the campervan, then saw his mum being forced into the passenger seat by his dad, who got behind the steering wheel and started the engine.

Jason panicked. In all the commotion, no one

had noticed him. He was going to be left here on his own.

Part of him thought that might be a good thing. Perhaps a nice couple hiking along the path would find him and become his new parents.

But another part of him knew that he was fantasising again and, like Stephen had told him, he needed to face reality.

The campervan began to move forward, rolling along beside the coastal path, picking up speed.

Suddenly terrified at the thought of being left alone, Jason ran forwards, towards the vehicle. He could see his parents in the front seats fighting. His mum was trying to grab the wheel while his dad was beating her hands away.

They weren't looking ahead. They couldn't see him as he ran towards them.

He waved his arms, trying to get their attention.

Just when he thought the vehicle might hit him and was about to get out of the way, his dad looked up and saw him. Jason moved to the side, avoiding the front of the campervan, but he hadn't realised that the wing mirrors stuck out from the side of the vehicle.

He felt a hard crack on his forehead as the solid, metal mirror holder struck him and staggered away, white stars blooming in his vision.

He looked back at the campervan in time to see it go over the edge of the cliff before the white flashes in his vision faded and everything became black.

CHAPTER
TWENTY-EIGHT

04:02

"Jason Graves," Battle said as Tony and Ryan entered his office, "is a hard man to track down. He made his fortune a couple of years ago, and then seems to have fallen off the face of the earth."

"What else do we know about him?" Tony asked.

"He was orphaned when his family went over that cliff and spent the rest of his childhood in the system, moving from foster home to foster home."

"Not a stable upbringing," Tony observed.

"No, but he did well out of it. Degrees in computer programming and engineering. Millionaire at twenty, thanks to some app he developed."

"What about the campervan incident?" Tony said. "The papers said his father killed the family and himself."

"The papers say a lot of things." The DCI tapped his finger on a stack of papers on his desk. "There were two eyewitnesses at the scene. A couple who'd chosen the wrong day to hike the coastal path. They saw Jason run in front of the campervan, causing the vehicle to swerve and go over the cliff."

"Bloody hell," Ryan said. "It was his fault they died."

Battle nodded. "Looks like it."

"So why is he taking it out on Dani?"

"Because it's all twisted around in his mind," Tony told him. "He doesn't blame himself for causing the accident. He blames Dani and Greg because they released his father from custody. It's a coping mechanism. Also, he was injured at the scene, so he might not remember what actually happened."

"None of that matters at the moment," Battle said. "We need to get Summers back. We need to know where she is."

There was a knock at the door and one of the female support staff entered. "We found three properties owned by Jason Graves, sir." She gave the DCI a sheet of paper and left.

Battle scrutinised the paper in is hand. "A flat in Chelsea, an office in central London, and a warehouse."

"Where's the warehouse?" Tony asked.

Battle shrugged. "There isn't an address. Just a set of coordinates." He marched to the door and opened it. "Where's this bloody warehouse?" he shouted at the support team. "Why isn't there an address?"

"It's on an island, sir," someone told him.

"That's it," Tony said. "He took Dani by boat. It's the island."

"I want details on this place now!" Battle shouted at the support team.

He came back into the office. "You know how to pin down coordinates," he said, passing the paper to Ryan. "Where is this?"

"I'll need a map, sir."

"Well get one, then."

Ryan left the office in a hurry.

The DCI glanced at the clock on the wall. "Less than four hours left."

"We'll get there in time," Tony said, wishing he felt as confident as he sounded.

Battle stormed out of the office. "Ryan! Have you found it yet?"

Tony followed.

Ryan was poring over a large map at his desk, using rulers to pinpoint the coordinates of the island. "Got it!" he said. "Horseshoe Island, off the Northumberland coast."

"I want every boat we can get our hands on," Battle told the support team. "Commandeer them from local fishermen if we have to. And I want every available chopper fuelled up and ready to get us to that island."

"We'll need a search warrant," Ryan said.

"Sod that. An officer is in danger. Ryan,

you're in the chopper with me. You too, doctor."

Tony nodded. He felt adrenaline coursing through his veins. This was going to happen. They were going to rescue Dani.

"There are a number of buildings on Horseshoe Island," Nick Evans, a member of the support team said. He had a satellite image on his screen. It showed a small cluster of structures located at the centre of a small island.

"We'll split into teams," Battle said. "I want everyone in the briefing room. Now."

Before following the DCI, Tony went over to the screen and examined the satellite image closely. The buildings were indistinct. Nothing more than grey squares.

"Can you find out what these buildings are? Floor plans, maybe?" he asked Nick.

The support team officer nodded confidently. "I'll try."

"Good man." Tony turned and was about to follow the others to the briefing room when he saw Chris Toombs rush onto the floor. The technician looked harried.

"What brings you up here?" Tony asked.

Toombs held his phone up so Tony could see the website on the screen.

The timer above the *Detective in Danger* square had changed. It read, *0:58*.

Less than an hour.

"No," Tony said, feeling a sudden hollowness in

his stomach. "We had four hours left. What happened?"

"It just changed. It went to one hour."

Tony shook his head, unwilling to believe the GameMaster had stolen their time. Why was he changing the rules of his own game?

Toombs looked at the image on Nick Evans' screen. "What's this?"

"That's Horseshoe Island," Tony said. "That's where he's got Dani."

Toombs face became ashen. "He probably has an alert set up if anyone uses the island as a search term. He knows we've found him."

"That's why he changed the rules," Tony said. "There's no time for a briefing. We have to get to that island now."

He sprinted toward the briefing room, hoping it wasn't already too late to save Dani.

CHAPTER
TWENTY-NINE

0:52

When the timer above the door changed, Dani felt a stab of fear in her chest. She had less than an hour before she had to face whatever the GameMaster had planned for her.

She heard a *click*, and then his came voice through the speakers.

"Your friends in the Murder Force are quite clever. They know where we are."

She felt a wave of relief wash over her and let out a sigh of relief. They were on their way here. There was a glimmer of hope.

"I suppose you think they're going to save you. They're not. I'm in control of this game. Don't forget that. It will take your friends more than an hour to get here and by then, the cameras will already be rolling."

She clenched her fists in anger. He had this whole thing rigged in his favour. She'd forgotten that.

"Let me go," she said. "Whatever you think I've done, you're mistaken. I don't even know who you are."

"I wouldn't expect you to remember me, detective. It was a long time ago when you and your partner destroyed my family with your actions."

She shook her head. "I don't know what you're talking about."

"Greg said exactly the same thing before he died. As I watched him drown, I realised he had no idea of the sin that had condemned him. No recollection of the tragedy he'd caused. But you'll remember. I'm going to make sure of that."

The door buzzed and opened inwards just enough that Dani could see lights flickering to life in the room beyond.

She remained on the bed.

"Go through the door, detective."

"Why? So you can kill me?"

He sighed. *"Look at the timer. There are forty-six minutes to go before your live feed begins. The contents of the room beyond your cell are just there to jog your memory."*

She considered her options and realised she didn't have any. If the GameMaster wanted to kill her, he could do so at any time. She'd seen the traps he'd constructed. This cell and the room beyond the door were probably rigged in some way. They could probably be filled with poison gas or flooded with water.

She might as well see what awaited her in the next room.

Getting up off the bed, she went to the door and pulled it open fully, revealing a room larger than the cell she was standing in.

The room was devoid of furniture but the walls were festooned with photos and pieces of paper.

Dani stepped over the threshold and the cell door swung shut behind her. She heard a *click* as it locked.

The papers on the wall were all copies of news articles from various papers. They were all related to an incident that had occurred twelve years ago.

SCARBOROUGH MAN KILLS FAMILY AND SELF

MAN DRIVES OVER CLIFF EDGE WITH FAMILY IN VEHICLE

RONALD GRAVES KILLS HIMSELF AND FAMILY IN CAMPERVAN TRAGEDY

The photographs on the wall were pictures of a woman and three children. They'd all been taken at campsites, or by the sea.

Dani knew this family. She remembered being called out to the Graves house in the middle of the night with Greg. She also remembered the tragedy that took place the following day.

A *click*, and then, *"You killed them, detective. You and your partner killed them all."*

She shook her head in defiance of the GameMaster's accusation. "No, we didn't."

"That's a lie. If you hadn't released Ronald Graves from the police station, that family would still be alive."

Dani searched her memory. She remembered that one boy had survived the tragedy. The boy she'd seen on the stairs in the Graves' residence the night before.

"Jason," she said. "You're Jason Graves."

Silence. Then, *"So you remember me."*

"Of course I do. I won't ever forget what happened to your family."

"The guilt eats away at you, doesn't it?"

"I'm not guilty of anything, Jason. We had to release your father because your mother wouldn't press charges."

"Liar!"

"It's true. She spoke to Greg on the phone before you all left in the campervan. She was running away from your father. She didn't want to be involved in legal proceedings."

"It doesn't matter. You knew what he was capable of, and you released him."

She wasn't sure why he'd said that. The papers may have reported that Ronald Graves had killed himself and his family on purpose, but Jason knew the truth, didn't he? He'd been at the scene, after all.

"You father didn't kill anyone, Jason. What happened was a terrible accident."

"No, it wasn't," he said with conviction. *"He killed them. Everyone knows that. It was in the papers."*

"They reported a story that would sell more papers. It wasn't the truth. Your father swerved to avoid running you over and accidentally drove over the edge of a cliff."

"No!"

"It's true. There were witnesses. They saw what happened. You don't remember it clearly because you banged your head on the campervan's wing mirror. You were unconscious in the hospital for twelve hours."

"You're lying. You let him go and he killed my family. I spent my childhood in foster homes because of you. I was brought up by strangers."

"I'm sorry that happened to you, but—"

"I tried to move on from it. Tried to forget what you and your partner did to my family. I worked hard. Became successful. But the hatred festered inside. Always there, beneath the surface. And then, one day, I read in the papers that Greg Hughes has rescued a homeless man from drowning. Not only that, you're on the TV rescuing women from a serial killer. How do you think that made me feel? You could save these people, but I had to suffer a life of loneliness and abuse because you couldn't save my family."

When Dani realised how irrational his thinking

was, she knew she had no chance of talking her way out of this. As far as Jason was concerned, she and Greg were to blame for everything bad that had happened in his life. He'd already exacted his revenge on Greg, and now it was her turn.

She looked about the room for the timer. There wasn't one in here.

"How long do I have left?" she asked.

"Twenty-two minutes. Then the world will watch as you are punished for your sins."

"I'm not responsible for anyone's death," she insisted.

There was a moment of silence and then he said, *"You soon will be."*

CHAPTER
THIRTY

0:13

As the helicopter raced above the coastline, Tony gripped the edges of his seat. The pilot had already made it clear that they wouldn't get to Horseshoe Island before the countdown timer reached zero.

Sitting next to Tony, Battle had a stoic expression on his face as he watched the landscape rush beneath them.

Ryan was also looking out of the helicopter window, but his attention was directed at the sea and the distant horizon.

No one spoke. After boarding the chopper and taking their seats, they had all become lost in their own thoughts.

Tony had spent most of the time trying to work

out what the live feed was going to show when it went live.

A tablet lay on the floor at his feet, its screen displaying the website which would shortly broadcast an image of Dani. It might be the last time he saw her alive.

0:11

Tony gripped the seat even harder. He felt useless. His friend was in danger, and there was nothing he could do. Whatever was about to happen, Dani was going to have to face it alone.

"Can't this thing go any faster?" Battle said. His voice came through the headset built into the flight helmet Tony wore.

"We're going as fast as we can, sir," the pilot replied.

"Well it's not bloody fast enough."

Although he didn't say it, Tony had known they didn't have enough time, ever since the timer had changed to one hour. That single hour hadn't been an arbitrary on the GameMaster's part. He'd chosen it because he knew it didn't give them enough time to save Dani.

As usual, the GameMaster held all the aces while Murder Force's hand was useless.

Unable to look at the tablet and the damned counter any longer, Tony shifted his attention to a file on Jason Graves that had been hastily put together by the support team.

Jason's upbringing had been anything but ideal. He'd been a troubled child. That was understandable, given the fact that he'd seen his entire family die, and probably knew, deep down, that he'd been the cause of the tragedy that had taken their lives.

Despite bouncing from foster home to foster home, Jason had somehow excelled in his studies and, after earning two degrees, had started a company that created apps. The company had been called Beyond the Graves, and its motto had been *Make your day great*, the same words Jason had written on the letter to Thomas Rayburn.

He'd purchased Horseshoe Island with his profits from Beyond the Graves, and had employed a number of construction firms to build a warehouse and other buildings, as well as a dock for his boat and a helipad.

Tony checked the pages for any mention of a helicopter. According to the support team's hurried research, Jason had a pilot's licence and owned a Bell 206B Jet Ranger helicopter. Was that how he hoped to avoid capture? Was he going to kill Dani and then escape in the chopper?

Tony showed the page to Battle and pointed at the part that said there was a helipad on the island.

"He might try to escape that way," he said into the flight helmet's built-in mic.

The DCI nodded once and cast a wary glance at the tablet on the floor.

0:04

Ryan, probably sensing the DCI's nervousness, asked, "How far out are the boats, guv?"

"Too far. We'll get there before they do."

Ryan nodded and sighed. "So, we'll be first on the scene."

Tony didn't want to contemplate everything that entailed. If Dani was dead, it would be them who found her.

Someone would have to tell Dani's daughter.

He decided not to dwell on the subject. His thoughts were becoming too morbid. He needed to keep his wits about him in case there was a chance —no matter how slim—that Dani might get out of this alive.

When he looked back at the tablet, there was less than a minute left.

Tony gritted his teeth, his eyes glued to the screen.

The timer reached zero and the live feed began.

CHAPTER
THIRTY-ONE

0:00

"It's time," the GameMaster's voice said through the speakers.

Dani tensed, ready for anything.

A door at the far side of the room slid aside, revealing a flight of stone steps leading up into darkness.

"I said, it's time," Jason repeated.

Dani didn't move. She refused to be rushed. The longer she stalled, the more time the others had to get here. Jason had said they'd found out where she was. If that was true, Battle and the others were on their way here now.

She heard a hissing sound coming from above her head. She looked up. Smoke drifted down out of a vent in the ceiling. When it reached her, it made her gag.

The room would soon be full of it. She had no choice. She had to move.

Holding her breath, she strode through the open doorway and stood at the foot of the stone steps. The door slid shut behind her, making sure she had nowhere to retreat to. She could only go forward.

The stairs ascended to a closed, metal hatch. Dani went up to the hatch and pushed against it. The hatch opened. Dani squinted her eyes against sudden sunlight and climbed through the hatch into a grassy area.

She looked around, realising she was on an island that was vaguely the shape of a crescent moon. She estimated the distance from one end to the other to be no more than a couple of miles. She could see the mainland in the distance and estimated the island to be ten miles offshore.

Several buildings huddled together some distance from her position. The rooms she'd just come from had been built underground, beneath a grassy field.

The only other thing of interest was a small helicopter sitting on a helipad beyond the buildings.

She looked around, at the field in which she stood. There were no traps that she could see. There was, however, a cardboard box a few feet to her left.

She heard a low buzz and saw a drone hovering in the air above her. A flashing red light indicated that it was filming her.

"Open the box, detective." The GameMaster's voice came from a speaker on the drone. *"When you see what's inside, you'll understand what you have to do."*

Dani swallowed and regarded the cardboard box. It looked innocent enough, but there could be any number of deadly devices inside.

She hesitated. Was the GameMaster's plan for her something so simple as a booby-trapped box?

"Open the box. There's something inside you need to see."

Dani didn't move.

"Someone's life depends on you opening that box, detective."

Her most basic instinct—to protect others—spurred her into action. She knelt next to the box and examined it. It wasn't sealed. She could see a computer tablet inside. That was all. Nothing else.

Reaching inside and taking the tablet out, she was surprised when the device flickered into life. The screen showed two people—a young man and a young woman—chained to a rocky wall. Their heads were drooped and their features were obscured by shadows. Water lapped about their knees.

As Dani looked more closely at the couple, her blood ran cold.

Charlie. The girl on the screen was Charlie.

And now that she realised she was looking at her daughter, she recognised the young man as well. Charlie's boyfriend. Elliot.

Dani tried to speak. To demand that Jason let

them go. But the words lodged in her throat and refused to come out.

She looked up at the drone imploringly.

"Where are they?" she managed.

"There's a cave on the north side of the island. The tide fills it completely. And the tide is coming in. You don't have time to save both of them."

"You bastard!" she shouted at the drone. Tears filled her eyes. Her chest tightened.

"Look under the box."

She kicked the box furiously. It flew across the grass and came to rest some distance away.

On the ground at Dani's feet lay a metal ring full of keys.

Dani picked it up. The keys were identical. Dozens of them hung from the ring.

"Perhaps you'll make the right choice," the Game-Master said.

She darted her gaze about. She had no idea which way was north.

"Turn to your right."

She did so. She was facing the far end of the island.

"That's where the cave is. Tick tock, detective."

Dani sprinted over the grass, the keys jangling in her hand as she pumped her arms. The drone followed, buzzing through the air behind her.

As she ran, her eyes streamed with tears. She knew there was no way to win Jason's game. He had told her that she was here to atone for her sins. He wouldn't let her simply rescue her daughter and

Elliot, and then leave. He intended to kill her. Of that, she was certain.

She tried not to think of how this day was going to end. She had to focus on her immediate task. She had to try to save lives.

By the time she reached the edge of the island, her legs and lungs burnt. She gasped for breath. Her racing heartbeat thrummed in her ears.

A low cliff swept down to a rocky shoreline that was already being overwhelmed by the sea. Large boulders were half-submerged in the roiling water. If there was a cave down there, it would soon be underwater.

She scrambled down the cliffside. The drone followed, hovering over the waves, its camera pointed towards her as she descended the rocks to the angry sea.

When she reached the water, she stood thigh-deep in it, searching the base of the cliff for an opening while crashing waves drenched her with cascades of salty spray.

She spotted a dark crack in the rock face that might be the cave she was looking for, and waded through the waves towards it, praying it wasn't just a fissure in the rock.

When she reached it, she peered inside. Light bulbs housed in protective cages had been hung there, illuminating a tunnel that ran deep into the cliff. No doubt there were cameras in there, as well. This was the place.

Dani squeezed into the opening and waded along

the natural tunnel, which was barely high enough for her to stand up straight. She ducked her head at places where the ceiling seemed to droop, and found herself half-crawling, half-swimming in sections where there was barely any headroom at all.

As she progressed deeper into the bowels of the cliff, she understood Jason's plan. She was moving into a trap. When the water completely filled this tunnel, there was no way she would be able to hold her breath long enough to swim back out.

But she couldn't turn back now. What if Charlie was chained up at the end of this tunnel? She couldn't leave her daughter to die down here alone.

Splashing through the water in the dim light provided by the bulbs, she reached the end of the tunnel, where the water poured into a small cavern.

Chained to the wall at the bottom of the cavern —fifteen feet below Dani and illuminated by a string of bulbs that hung from the cavern's ceiling—were Charlotte and Elliot.

"Charlie!" Dani shouted. Her voice reverberated around the enclosed space but Charlie didn't move. Her chin rested on her chest. Her hair obscured her face. The water was rising quickly and had already reached Charlie's waist.

Dani lowered herself down as much as she was able before the force of the water rushing through the tunnel swept her into the cavern.

She went under for a second, then righted herself and—spluttering—found her feet.

CHAPTER THIRTY-ONE

She lifted her daughter's head and wiped wet hair from her face.

"Charlie, can you hear me?"

Charlie groaned, but her eyes remained shut.

Dani checked Elliot's pulse. It was weak.

She returned her attention to her daughter. The heavy chains had been arranged so that they all interlocked into a mechanism on Charlie's chest. Dani frantically ran her fingers over the device, searching for some sort of release button, but all she found was a keyhole.

She still had the keys in her hand. She tried one. It fit into the hole but would not turn. She pulled it out and tried another, getting the same result.

Gritting her teeth against the frustration, anger, fear, and the cold, she tried another and then another. None of them worked.

The rising water now almost reached the bottom of the mechanism.

Dani told herself to calm down. If she panicked, she could blow this and her daughter would die.

Forcing herself to take a deep, slow breath, she remembered something the GameMaster had said when she'd found the keys.

Perhaps you'll make the right choice.

She remembered the sign Tony had read when faced with three identical cabins.

Choose wisely.

The GameMaster had set up the situation so Tony would think the choice related to the cabins.

But the cabins had been traps. The *wise* choice was elsewhere.

She held the keyring in her palm and inspected it. Were all these keys useless? Was this keyring a decoy?

Perhaps you'll make the right choice.

The right choice had nothing to do with this keyring, she was certain of it. The right choice lay elsewhere, just as it had been when Tony had rescued David Goddard.

She looked around the cavern for something—anything—out of place. All she could see in the stark light cast by the bulbs were rocks and water, and a camera watching her from overhead. There was nothing else here. No sign to indicate where she should look.

The right choice.

How literal had he been? Dani looked to her right, searching the rock wall for a ledge where a key might be hidden. There was nothing there but smooth rock.

She checked Charlie's right hand, alarmed at how cold and lifeless it felt, despite the fact that her daughter was clearly alive.

There was no key attached to the cold flesh.

Dani slid her fingers into the right pocket of Charlie's jeans. Her fingers contacted with something metal. She pinched it between her forefinger and thumb and brought it out of the water.

A key.

With fingers that shook from cold and fear, she slid it into the keyhole on the device and turned it.

Click

The chains dropped into the water and Charlie slumped forward. Dani caught her and held her daughter close.

She looked over at Elliot. If she used the key—which was now underwater somewhere, still attached to the mechanism—to unlock his chains, he'd drop into the water and drown. The chains were holding him upright.

There was no way she could carry both Elliot and Charlie through the tunnel.

"I'll come back for you, Elliot," she said. "I need to get Charlie to safety." She didn't know if he could hear her or not, but if he could, she wanted to reassure him that she hadn't forgotten about him and would be back.

She had to move fast. It wouldn't be long before the tunnel became totally submerged.

Dani managed to heave Charlie's limp body into the tunnel mouth and—aided by the buoyancy of the water—drag her to the first section where the ceiling was so low that swimming underwater was the only option.

"Hold your breath, Charlie," she whispered, her teeth chattering. She felt so cold, as if the relentless surge of the sea was dragging all the life out of her body.

She gently pushed her daughter's head underwater and went under herself, pulling Charlie behind her as she scrambled for the next pocket of air.

When she found it, she sucked in a deep breath and checked Charlie. When she didn't detect any sign that her daughter was breathing, she slapped Charlie's cold cheeks gently.

"Charlie!"

Charlie groaned and her eyelids fluttered.

Dani felt an overwhelming urge to cry with relief but suppressed it. They weren't out of danger yet. There were more sections of the tunnel that would be completely submerged, and some of them would be longer than the one they'd just passed through.

"Hold on, Charlie. We'll make it out of here."

She swam further along the tunnel. Even this area, where the ceiling was higher, would soon be sealed completely by the rising water. Dani had to hurry. Once she got Charlie out, she had to come back for Elliot.

Reaching the next submerged section, she pushed Charlie underwater and scrambled over the rocks, dragging her daughter behind her.

When she emerged into an air pocket, she was distressed to find the water almost reaching the ceiling. She had barely enough room to take and breath and hold Charlie's head out of the water for a moment before she had to dive again.

She felt along the ceiling with one hand as she moved forwards, holding Charlie with the other. Her lungs began to ache and still she hadn't found an air pocket.

Trying to remember the sections of the tunnel where she had been forced to crouch on her way in, and how long they were, she began to panic.

Hadn't there been a long stretch of low ceiling, where she'd had to crouch for at least a minute? She'd been walking then, wading through the water. Now, she was crawling beneath the surface, with Charlie's limp body. How long would that minute stretch? Would she be able to hold her breath for that long? Would Charlie?

She tried to move as fast as she could, fighting the current that attempted to drive her back. Charlie's body felt so heavy, despite the buoyancy provided by the water. Dani's lungs cried out for air.

When she was sure she wasn't going to make it, her hand broke the surface of the water. Dani tried to stand, pulling Charlie upright.

She gasped in a lungful of salty air. She could see the cave mouth and the bright sky beyond.

"Charlie, we made it!"

Hooking an arm over her daughter's chest and pulling her close, Dani swam for the opening in the cliff face. The waves tried to push her back, but she fought them with everything she had, until she was out of the cave and among the rocks on the shore.

She found a large rock with a smooth surface and heaved Charlie onto it. Her daughter lay on her back, her face turned to the sky, her eyes closed.

Dani clambered onto the rock and leaned over Charlie, feeling for a pulse in her daughter's neck.

She couldn't feel anything.

"Charlie!"

She straddled Charlie's unmoving body and pressed the heels of her hands into her daughter's chest rhythmically.

"Come on," she whispered, hot tears running down her cheeks, mingling with the cold, salty spray that hit her face as the waves crashed around her.

She heard a buzzing sound somewhere over the sea and turned to see if the drone was there. The sound wasn't coming from the drone, which was nowhere to be seen. Dani realised it was the sound of distant helicopter rotor blades chopping through the air.

Had Jason made his escape before the others got here? Had he run like the coward he was?

Charlie's body convulsed and she opened her mouth, spewing water over the rock.

Dani breathed a sigh of relief.

Charlie continued to cough, her body racked with spasms as her lungs expelled the water she'd inhaled.

The helicopter was closer now. Dani could see the blue and yellow paintwork glinting in the sun. A police helicopter.

As she watched, the chopper descended until it hovered no more than ten feet above the waves. Someone jumped out, into the sea, and swam towards her.

The chopper gained height and continued on its way, flying over the cliffs.

The swimmer got closer, and Dani saw that it was Ryan. He wore a red backpack, which he passed to Dani when he got close enough.

"There are blankets in there, and other first aid equipment, if you need it."

Dani wanted to hug him, to cry on his shoulder and feel his strong arms around her. But she couldn't. Elliot was still in the cave.

"Elliot's still in there," she said, pointing at the cave mouth.

Ryan nodded. "I know. We saw the video." He breaststroked over to the cave and entered it, disappearing from view.

"Mum," Charlie said, her teeth chattering. "I'm cold.:"

Dani unzipped the waterproof backpack and took out a red emergency blanket. She sat her daughter up and draped it over her shoulders.

A second helicopter was approaching in the distance. This one was red and white, the colour of the Coastguard.

Dani stood up and waved her arms at it. When it got closer, she saw the rescue basket hanging beneath its body, and the operator leaning out of the open door.

The helicopter hovered above them and the basket began to lower.

Dani grabbed it when it was within reach and guided it to the rock's surface.

"Get in," she told her daughter.

Charlie shook her head. "I'm not going anywhere without Elliot."

"Charlie, get in."

"I need to see Elliot. I need to know he's okay."

"Ryan's gone to get him."

"I'm not leaving until I see him."

Charlie, get in. Now."

Her daughter sighed and nodded hesitantly before climbing into the basket and lying down.

Dani looked up at the operator and gave him a thumbs up. The basket was reeled in, rising smoothly into the air with Charlie inside.

Dani watched as her daughter was bundled into the helicopter. She closed her eyes and whispered, "Thank you." She had no idea to whom she was giving thanks. She just felt relieved that Charlie was safe that she had to express her gratitude in some way.

Ryan appeared, coughing and spluttering. He looked at Dani with eyes that told her everything she needed to know before he even spoke. He hadn't been able to rescue Elliot.

"The tunnel's totally flooded," he said. "It's impossible to get through without SCUBA equipment."

Dani nodded solemnly. She'd given her thanks too early. And when she got into the Coastguard helicopter, she was going to have to tell Charlie that her boyfriend hadn't made it.

If the GameMaster had meant to punish her, then he'd done his job perfectly.

Dani would ask herself every day if she should have done something differently in that cave.

"He's won," she said to Ryan as the DC climbed onto the rock next to her.

"What do you mean?"

"He wanted to prove that the police can't save everyone and he's done that."

"Dani, he probably expected all three of you to die in there. You did a damn fine job of surviving. And you got your daughter out."

"It's not enough," she said, staring at the flooded cave and shaking her head. "It's not enough."

CHAPTER
THIRTY-TWO

The helicopter carrying Battle and Tony regained altitude after dropping off Ryan and swooped over the cliffs towards the cluster of buildings at the centre of the island.

"We haven't got any backup," Battle said to Tony over the headset. "It's up to us to make sure the bastard doesn't get away."

Tony nodded. He had no intention of letting Jason Graves get away with what he'd done. He'd watched the live feed of Dani and her daughter almost drowning, and from what he could see on the tablet's screen right now—Ryan swimming into the cave with a doubtful look on his face—he wasn't sure Elliot was going to make it out alive.

He'd also worked out that the timer changing from four hours to one hour hadn't been Jason's reaction to them searching the Net for Horseshoe Island at all. The sudden time shift had been planned all along. It had to be, because Jason had timed everything with the tides.

Even in his own game, the GameMaster hadn't played fair.

"Sir." The pilot's voice came over the headsets. "You need to see this." He was pointing at the island below.

Battle and Tony peered out of the windows. Below them, on a patch of grass near the buildings, a white banner had been staked to the ground so that it pointed up at them.

Painted on the banner in black paint were the words, PEOPLE'S LIVES ARE IN DANGER INSIDE THE HOUSE.

Battle frowned. "What's he playing at now?"

"Probably buying time to get away," Tony said. "He knows we can't ignore it. We have to go inside and check."

"Get us down to the house," Battle told the pilot. "But keep an eye on that helicopter. If it goes anywhere, follow it."

As the DCI spoke, the Bell Ranger lifted up from the helipad into the air.

"He's making a run for it. Go after him."

"What about the people in the house?" Tony asked. He wasn't even sure there *were* people in the house, but as he'd already said, they had to check.

"Bloody hell!" Battle was in obvious turmoil.

The Bell Ranger turned so that its nose pointed north and then flew in that direction, away from the island.

As it flew over the sea, black smoke began to pour out of the engine.

"He's in trouble, sir," the pilot said.

The Bell Ranger spun, enveloped by the smoke, and descended towards the sea.

"Maybe we'll catch him after all," Battle said. "He's not going far."

Before it reached the waves, the helicopter exploded. It became a bright orange fireball as it plummeted into the sea.

The fiery wreckage hit the water and began to sink, flames licking the air and black smoke rising up into the sky above the point of impact.

"No one could survive that," Battle said grimly. "Get us down to that house," he told the pilot."

The pilot took them down and landed gently on the grass near the house. Tony and Battle got out and rushed to the house, ducking their heads as they passed beneath the spinning rotor blades.

The house was modern, consisting mainly of glass and metal. The huge windows probably offered a panoramic view of the island from inside the house, but they were tinted and didn't allow Battle or Tony to see inside.

A tall, slim, metal door offered access to the house but was closed.

Battle pulled it open and went inside. Tony followed, all too aware that Jason's favourite method of killing was to lay traps for the unwary. He only hoped that he and Battle weren't rushing into one of those traps right now.

The room they stood in was sparsely furnished with nothing more than a white, leather sofa and chair. A huge TV was bolted to the wall over a faux fireplace.

An open doorway revealed a large kitchen with modern, stainless-steel appliances. A flight of stairs led up to the next level.

"I'll check upstairs," Battle said. "You take the kitchen."

Tony entered the kitchen carefully, hearing Battle's footsteps, heavy on the stairs and the floor above.

The only thing of interest in here—other than the top-end cooker and fridge—was a closed door. Tony approached it and knocked.

"Is there anybody in there?"

No answer. With each passing minute, Tony was more certain of his theory that Jason had sent them in here to buy himself time to get away. Not that it mattered now. The GameMaster had gone down in flames. Literally.

Tony opened the door. Metal stairs led down to a basement. Lights flickered on down there, probably activated by a motion sensor that had detected Tony at the top of the stairs.

He went down to the brightly lit room and whistled in appreciation when he saw the equipment down there. Banks of servers stood against one wall, humming gently. Half a dozen state of the art computers sat on a large, metal, crescent-shaped desk.

Tony walked over to the desk and examined the computers. They were on, their screens bright. Every screen displayed the same thing: a white background with large, black numbers counting down.

0:02.12

A countdown.

With two minutes left.

Tony turned and ran back up the stairs. "Battle!"

The DCI was coming down the stairs at a leisurely pace. "Nothing upstairs. You were right. There's nobody—"

"We've got to get out of here. Now!"

Battle frowned. "What's up?"

"The computers in the basement are counting down."

"Bloody hell. Let's go."

They ran out of the door and across the grassy area.

Seeing them running from the house, the helicopter pilot started the engines. They whirred into life and the rotor blades began to turn.

"Get us out of here!" Battle shouted as he and Tony clambered into the aircraft.

The pilot nodded and pulled back on the flight yoke, lifting them into the air.

The house exploded. Glass and metal blew outwards as a bright orange fireball engulfed the building. The helicopter, still rising, shook in the blast wave and Tony felt as if his teeth were rattling inside his head.

Black smoke plumed into the sky from a twisted metal skeleton which was all that remained of the house.

"There goes all the bloody evidence," Battle observed, shaking his head as he looked down at the burning ruins. He sat back in his seat. "Well, I suppose it doesn't matter. The so-called Game-Master won't be playing any more games."

Tony turned his attention from the house to the wreckage of the helicopter in the sea. When the police boats arrived, they would have divers aboard. What was left of the downed helicopter would be retrieved, along with Jason Graves' body.

The more he thought about it, the more sceptical Tony became that the divers would find anything. Jason had planned everything meticulously. Had he also planned the helicopter crash? Had he been on the chopper when it had left the island, or had he been elsewhere?

"What's wrong?" Battle said, seeing Tony's concerned look.

Tony looked at the DCI and grimaced. "You don't think he's...*escaped*, do you?"

"What? Don't say that, doctor."

Tony sighed. "I just think..." he tried to find the right words. "He has this entire thing planned out to every last detail and then he falls foul of a fault on his helicopter? It doesn't ring true."

"Are you saying you don't think he was on that helicopter when it blew up?"

"We know he rigged the house to blow, so why not the helicopter as well?"

Battle pondered that for a moment. "Let's hope the divers find his body, then."

Tony nodded, gazing at the thread of smoke rising from the crashed helicopter.

Until the GameMaster's body was found, he was going to doubt that this was all over.

CHAPTER
THIRTY-THREE

Two Days Later

Dani stood on the moors, watching the morning sun burn off the fog that had settled over the landscape during the night.

Barney and Jack rambled over the heather together, occasionally breaking into a mad dash and chasing each other until they were exhausted and lay on the ground panting.

The sedative Radcliffe had fed them had worn off after a couple of hours, apparently. While she'd been a captive of the GameMaster, Barney and Jack had been recovering at the vets.

Dani wished she could be as carefree as the dogs. She'd spent the last two days with her nerves at breaking point. Jason Graves' body had not been found by the dive team. That didn't mean he hadn't been in the helicopter when it crashed, they had assured her. His body might have been swept away by the current, or been destroyed by the explosion.

She wasn't confident in those explanations, and she'd seen the same doubt in Tony's face when they'd been offered by the dive team.

If Jason Graves was still out there somewhere, would he leave her alone? After all, he'd proved his point, that the police couldn't save everyone. She'd failed to save Elliot, and the whole world had seen the events unfold.

Jason had also destroyed her life in another way. Charlie was no longer speaking to her. After spending a day in hospital, her daughter had returned to Birmingham. Her last words to her mother had been, "Don't bother calling me."

Dani had tried to explain that there was no way she could have dragged Charlie and Elliot through the flooding tunnel. That she had intended to go back for her daughter's boyfriend. But it was all to no avail. Charlie blamed her for Elliot's death.

It felt like the cruellest punishment the Game-Master could possibly have inflicted on her. Perhaps he'd planned it that way.

After her experience on the island, she'd been told to take a couple of days off by Battle. She was back at work tomorrow. Hopefully, some case or other would turn up that would take her mind off recent events.

And hopefully, Charlie would come around in time. Until then, Dani would give her daughter the space she needed, no matter how hard that was going to be.

"Come on, boys," she called to the dogs. They wheeled around and trotted through the heather to her side as she headed back to her cottage.

When she was in sight of her home, she saw a car parked on the road outside the cottage. She couldn't discern any details. The vehicle was nothing more than a dark shape, almost ethereal in the lifting fog. Her throat tightened and she stopped in her tracks, unable to move.

Had the GameMaster come for her? Had he escaped Horseshoe Island while she'd been busy on the shoreline and Battle and Tony had been searching the house for people that were never there?

Her phone rang. She took it out of her pocket and inspected the screen. It was Ryan.

"Ryan," she said. "I think there's someone—"

"It's me, guv. I can see you and the dogs on the moors. At least I think it's you. Hard to tell with all this fog. I'm fairly sure there's no one else around here with two big dogs that run around like lunatics, though."

"It's me," she said, relieved. She started walking again, the dogs following.

When she reached the road, Ryan was leaning against his Aston Martin. A full shopping bag sat on the bonnet.

"I thought I'd make you a proper breakfast. Thank you for the meal the other day."

"That was a microwaveable ready meal. Is that what you've got in the bag? A selection of ready meals?"

He shook his head. "I make a mean breakfast. This is all fresh ingredients. And a couple of treats for the dogs."

"How can I say no, then? Come in." She opened the cottage door. Barney and Jack barged inside. She and Ryan followed.

Ryan went to the kitchen and unpacked the contents of the bag onto the counter. Dani smiled. She knew why he was here. He'd seen how distressed she'd been in the Coastguard helicopter, seen the rift between her and Charlie. Despite his gruff exterior, he seemed to be sensitive to such things and the fact that he was here now, offering to cook her a meal, meant he had come to offer moral support.

She felt the edginess of the last two days fade into the background as she helped him find what he needed in the kitchen cupboards.

And when he shooed her out of the kitchen to let him get on with it, she sat on the window seat, watching the fog lift from the moors.

For a moment, she allowed herself to believe that everything was going to be okay.

CHAPTER
THIRTY-FOUR

Tony sat in *Sam's Café* with a plate of beans on toast and a mug of tea on the table in front of him. His appetite, which had been growing before the Game-Master case, seemed to have vanished.

For the past couple of days, he'd sustained himself on little more than toast and an occasional coffee. He'd come here—to his old haunt—to try and rekindle his love for food.

But it hadn't worked. He hadn't even touched the beans on toast.

He couldn't put his finger on what was wrong. He suspected that Jason Graves—aka the Game-Master—was still at large, in hiding somewhere, but that shouldn't affect his appetite like this.

He just felt as if something was missing from his life.

The obvious answer, of course, was Alina. She'd returned to the dig in Sussex, and Tony had realised for the first time that he didn't like returning to an empty flat after work. He missed her conversation, her presence.

He took a sip of the tea and set the mug back down, deciding he couldn't face the beans on toast. He'd go to work on an empty stomach and perhaps grab a sandwich from the canteen for lunch. Perhaps.

The bell above the door jangled. Tony was about to take a final sip of tea and leave when he felt a hand on his shoulder.

For a split second, he froze. Had the Game-Master somehow followed him here? Was Jason Graves about to begin another game, with Tony as a victim?

"I thought I'd find you here."

He turned in his seat. Alina stood there, smiling at him.

"What are you doing here?" he asked, bewildered. "You're supposed to be in Sussex."

She slipped into the seat opposite him. "You sounded so down, so I thought I'd come back and see you."

He didn't know what to say. She'd travelled over four hundred miles just because he sounded down. He felt tears well in his eyes.

She looked at him, concerned. "I did the right thing, yes?"

He nodded. "Yes." Reaching across the table, he took her hands in his. "Thank you."

She smiled. "So, do you think you can get the day off work?"

"I'm sure I can." Battle wouldn't object. Tony's last holiday had been cut short, after all.

"Good. I thought we might visit the *Jorvik Viking Centre*, since we didn't get a chance last time."

"Yes, great idea. You must be hungry after your journey. What would you like?"

"A salad sandwich will be fine."

He stood up and went to the counter to order the food. When he returned to the table, he took his phone out of his pocket. "I'd best call Battle and request the time off."

"You should eat your breakfast first, before it goes cold."

"Yes, I should." He began to tuck into the beans on toast. Nothing had ever tasted so good.

CHAPTER
THIRTY-FIVE

Lakeside Institution. Ontario, Canada

Jerry Bickerson parked his Ford Escape in the parking lot of the Lakeside Institution and got out, taking his suit jacket from the back seat and shrugging it on before grabbing his briefcase.

The night was cold, and he wished to God he was back in the bed he'd left an hour ago. He needed to tell his client that he didn't appreciate being called in the middle of the night. His wife, Betty, hadn't appreciated being woken up either, and had told Jerry to ignore the phone.

He wished he had. Then he wouldn't be at this God-forsaken place at this ungodly hour.

Telling himself he was going to take tomorrow off work and make it up to Betty somehow, he entered the Lakeside Institution—a place he'd visited many times before—and showed his ID to the guard behind the Plexiglass screen before signing in.

"Wait here," the guard said. "Someone will be along shortly to escort you."

Jerry nodded and took a seat on the scarred wooden bench that ran along the corridor wall, rubbing his eyes. The light in here was too bright for a man who had been tucked up in bed only an hour ago.

A buzz sounded and the door at the far end of the corridor opened. Charlie Lapointe, a guard Jerry knew well, popped his head around the door and said, "You want to come through, Jerry?"

Jerry didn't really want to, but now that he was here, he guessed he might as well get on with it. He stood, stretching his back which was sore from the long drive over here, and went through the door that led to the interior of the prison.

"He's got you running around late tonight, eh?" Charlie said as they walked together to an identical door which Charlie opened with a key card.

"Yeah, I guess so."

They stepped through and Charlie indicated a door on the left. "He's in there. Grumpy as always."

"No change there, then," Jerry said, opening the door and stepping into the room.

The room contained a single table and two chairs, on opposite sides. On one of the chairs sat Solomon Gantz. He was handcuffed to a steel bar that ran the length of the table.

Jerry was always surprised by Gantz's size. On

the day of his arrest, Gantz had been burly but now, he was massive. The orange, short-sleeved shirt he wore was stretched so tightly across his biceps and chest that Jerry wouldn't be surprised if the seams ripped and the muscles burst out, like when Bruce Banner transformed into the Incredible Hulk.

"Hi, Solomon," he said, taking a seat across from his client. "What can I do for you?"

Gantz regarded him with dark eyes that made Jerry think of a crow observing a piece of meat it was about to grab with its beak.

"I'm going to tell them what they want to know."

Jerry wasn't sure what Gantz was talking about. "Come again? What do they want to know?"

"Where the bodies are."

That took Jerry aback. The bodies of some of Gantz's victim had never been recovered. Gantz had steadfastly refused to give up their locations, revelling in the distress it caused the families of the missing girls.

So why had he changed his mind now? Jerry had never known Gantz to do anything for anyone. The man was motivated by two forces: personal gain, and destruction of others. He didn't have an altruistic bone in his body.

"Why do you want to do that?" Jerry asked.

"It's time," Gantz said enigmatically.

Jerry didn't know what to say to that. He was sure that the man sitting across the table—the man the paper had called the Lake Erie Ripper—was planning something dangerous.

"You're just going to tell them? You don't want anything in return?"

There is something I want. And as my lawyer, you're going to make sure I get it."

Jerry pursed his lips. He didn't like Gantz's tone, but he thought of the families who might get some kind of closure if their loved ones' remains were found.

"What do you want?" he said.

"I can't just tell them where the bodies are. My memory isn't that good. I need to *show* them where they are."

Jerry, who was sure that Gantz's memory was just fine, said, "Uh huh." So, this was all about getting out of the prison. He couldn't blame Gantz for wanting to get some fresh air. This place was stifling.

But if his client thought he was going to succeed in some sort of half-assed escape attempt, he hadn't reckoned on the might of the Ontario Police Department. They wouldn't let Gantz take a piss without at least five officers surrounding him.

"I'll see what I can do," he said.

Gantz nodded. "There's one more thing."

"Okay."

Gantz reached down and took something from his lap. He placed it on the table between them.

Jerry looked at it. A copy of the *Toronto Star*. The

headline on the front page read, *RIPPER PSYCHOLOGIST SAVES KIDNAPPED BOY IN BRITAIN.*

A grainy black and white photo showed the British psychologist, Tony Sheridan, pulling a young boy out of what looked like a hole in the ground.

Gantz pressed his finger against the photo, pressing it against the psychologist's head. "I'll show them where the bodies are on one condition. He has to be there too."

He looked up with those dark crow eyes and said, "I want to see Tony Sheridan."

THE END

OTHER BOOKS BY ADAM J. WRIGHT

Psychological Thrillers:

DARK PEAK (DCI Battle)

THE RED RIBBON GIRLS (DI Summers)

Urban Fantasy:

THE HARBINGER PI SERIES

LOST SOUL

BURIED MEMORY

DARK MAGIC

DEAD GROUND

SHADOW LAND

MIDNIGHT BLOOD

TWILIGHT HEART

FAERIE STORM

NIGHT HUNT

GRAVE NIGHT

FINAL MAGIC